Broken

Alyssa Nicole

To Karla,
          Thank you for your
Support and for being the best
Creative writing teacher. You
Changed me as a writer and I
am so greatful for you. I
wouldn't be the writer I am
today if I hadn't have taken
your class. I hope you
enjoy the story. ☺
          - Alyssa N. Wright

Isbn: 978-1-7357626-0-9

Broken

By: Alyssa Nicole

Cover Design By: JJ Nitka

Edited By: Patrick Vibreza

First Printed 2020

To all the aspiring writers.

You can do it!

Just start writing,

you will find your path along the way.

Acknowledgements

I want to thank everyone who has supported me on this four year journey of writing and growth. This being my first book, I have learned so much about the writing process and how much it takes to write a good book. I want to thank my parents for their help and patience as they let me bounce ideas off of them and always gave me honest feedback on ideas. Thanks to my editor, Patrick, for taking a chance and time on my book. Thank you to my cover designer, JJ, for your hard work and your patience with my back and forth ideas. You have a bigger role than you realize as people really do judge a book by its cover. And to my readers, thanks for taking a chance, hope you enjoy.

Broken

Chapter 1

I'm trying to stay open minded about this whole AA thing, but so far it just seems like a lot of complaining and sob stories. I mean I feel bad, for this guy who's talking, I mean I should be paying attention, this guy is pouring his heart out. But I keep getting distracted. *Did I unplug the toaster before I left?* I thought to myself. *Did I flush the toilet?* Jen hates when people don't flush the toilet.

"Well now that we all have shared, I invite our newest member, Kai, to share." The group leader says. As soon as he says my name, I snap to attention.

"Do you want me to stand or can I sit?" I ask, sitting up in my seat. It was so early, I was still half asleep. I probably should have gotten a coffee before this, but I was running late. I was going to grab some from the pot they had in the back, but some guy told me not to. He said that he wouldn't drink it unless you wanted to get food poisoning, because Linda doesn't know how to make a pot of coffee if the instructions slapped her in the face.

"Most people stay seated, but whichever makes you more comfortable. Tell us about yourself." He says patiently, then takes a sip of his coffee.

I stayed seated, "Hi, my name is Kai." I say, then the group utters a mumbled greeting. I continue "It has been nine hours and..." I check my phone "twelve minutes since my last drink. When I was a young girl, my mom used to tell me not to judge her because I would end up messed up just like she was. Well I guess in some ways she was right, here I am in a meeting. But she wasn't right in the ways she thought she would be. And hey, at least one of us is trying, at least I've never driven my car into a lake piss drunk." I say then go quiet.

"Why have you joined us today Kai?" The group leader asks after a long pause.

"Honestly?" I ask and he nods his head for me to continue. "Attending AA meetings is part of my probation. About myself? Umm, I have some training in MMA, so you know, don't try to fight me." I say with a chuckle then pause, this earns a laugh from the group. Then I continue, "I'm 24, it has been about two or three years now since I moved from New York to California. I'm a triplet, Peter and Henry are my twins; we come from a big family. I currently live in a house on the beach, with several roommates. My boyfriend and I basically live together. He doesn't even know I'm here right now; I snuck out early this morning. And honestly, that's about as much as you are gonna get. I'm required to show up to meetings, but nowhere does it say I gotta share."

"I understand that it can be hard to trust a group of strangers. But I assure you anything said in group is privileged. But that's it for today, hopefully we'll see everyone soon."

I walk outside into the crisp cold morning air, pass the smokers and coffee drinkers, then take a cab home. I sneak into the house, quietly jog up the stairs, then slowly crawl back into bed after kicking off my clothes. Jay was still asleep. The sunlight peeked through the cracks of the curtains, showing beams of light with floating dust specs in the air. I gently turn onto my side facing towards him. His back is towards me, he is shirtless, just lying in his boxers. I lightly trace a line down between his shoulder blades. He stirs and I pull my hand back tucking it into my chest. He rolls onto his other side, facing me and takes a deep breath but doesn't say anything, falling back asleep. I look at his tattoo sleeve on his right arm that reaches from his shoulder down to his wrist and the little ones on his fingers. I look up to find he is awake and looking at me. He reaches forward and pulls me into him. "Good morning, gorgeous." He says with a smile and that rugged morning voice.

I put my forehead against his chest and breathe in his smell. He grabs my chin, tilts my head upward and kisses me.

There was a knock on the door and he groans, then we pulled apart.

"Come in," I yell. It was one of my roommates Dakota.

"Hey Kai, oh sorry didn't know Jay was here". He says and looks away quickly.

Why wouldn't he? I thought to myself. *He's here most nights.*

"It's fine bro, we need to get up anyway. She just wants to lay in bed all day." Jay says with a wink at me.

"Ok uhh..." Dakota shifts his weight uncomfortably. I roll my eyes and ask, "What did you need Dakota?"

"Oh right. Um. There's these two kids here to see you, Milos and uhh, Sasha."

"You serious?" I ask.

"How would I just make that up?" He says with an annoyed sigh, as he crosses his arms across his chest.

"Are they alone?" I ask.

"Yup. You know them? Or you want me to tell them they got the wrong address?" Dakota asks, pointing behind him with his thumb.

"No, let them in. They are two of my younger brothers." I say. I look at Jay. "What are they doing here? They are fifteen and thirteen and live in New York."

"Were you expecting them?" Dakota asks.

"No, I haven't talked to them in months. How did they get here by themselves?"

Dakota leaves and Jay gets up, pulling on his jeans, "Only one way to find out."

Chapter 2

We get dressed and walk down stairs. Dakota had let the boys in, and his girlfriend, Julie, was in the kitchen, making the boys some eggs and French toast.

"Thanks Julie. You didn't have to do that." I tell her.

Jen, one of my roommates, calls from down the hall, "Don't tell her that! Cause then she wouldn't have extras for us!"

I yell back down the hall, "You know how to make French toast and eggs!"

She laughs and yells back, "But they are better when she makes them!"

Julie finishes making breakfast and hands the boys their plates. They turn towards me with sheepish smiles.

"What do you say to Julie?" I ask them.

"Thank you for breakfast Julie." They both say.

I guide them to the table and pour both of them something to drink; orange juice for Milos, milk for Sasha. Then I grab the syrup from the pantry, setting it on the table.

I look to the corner where I see their bags full of clothes and stuff. I shake my head and ask; "How did you get from New York to California all by yourselves?"

"Mom's new boyfriend, Javi, buys tickets to places all the time for his work. He left his laptop out with his account unlocked, we simply booked two first class seats." They looked very proud of themselves.

"How creative of you. Though I'm sure mom will make you pay him back. If she's serious about this guy that is."

"It's fifty-fifty at this point." Sasha says after a drink of milk.

I get up, "Done?" They nod their heads. I put their plates in the sink and they follow me putting their glasses in the sink as well. Julie grabs the plates and starts to wash them, I squeeze her shoulder as I walk past. I smile and grab their shoulders from behind, leading them out front, "Let's go outside and talk." We walk out to the front porch and sit on the porch swing, while Jay leans on the railing.

"You can stay the weekend in the guest room but after that we have to get you home." I tell them.

"Why can't we stay with you?" Milos asks with a sad puppy dog face.

"Because you live and go to school in NYC. Not to mention I'm not your legal guardian." I inform them.

"But mom's new boyfriend sucks! He keeps trying to boss us around. He's not our dad." Milos says a little louder than necessary.

"This isn't a question. You have to go home. Don't you think mom is worried about where you are? And not to mention if Mom files missing persons reports on you, we could all get in trouble with the cops." I say seriously.

I look at Jay and he just laughs and gives me the *I'm not getting involved* look.

"Mom has been on a bender all week. She probably hasn't even noticed we are gone." Milos says sadly.

"Who's been taking care of you? Jack said that mom went to rehab before he left New York." I asked confused.

"That's where she met her new boyfriend. Once they met, neither of them lasted on the rehab road too long." Sasha says looking at his hands in his lap.

"What about dad, Milos? Why don't you go stay with him? And Sasha, didn't your dad just buy a new house?" I ask them.

Milos laughs. "Yeah sure, go stay with dad. I am sure a social worker would love that. He's on parole and with his record, that wouldn't look too good".

"My dad is too busy with his new family; his new wife just had twins. He doesn't have time for me." Sasha chimes in looking away off towards the street. I put an arm around his shoulder and kiss the side of his head.

"I'm sorry. You know I love both of you," I say while putting my other arm around Milos. "but you can't stay here. I'll call Carson and see what he wants to do.

"You mean your ex-boyfriend Carson? What good will he do?" Milos asks, giggling.

"Don't be cheeky, Milos. You know I mean our older brother Carson. And that ex's name was Carter not Carson. You know that, you little dork." I tell him.

Before they can protest again, a truck pulls up and Taj, from our "motorcycle club", gets out. "The boss wants to see you." Taj barks out.

"It needs to wait. I'm dealing with my two runaways here." I reply with a sigh.

"No, now. It's not a question Kai. Get in the truck or I will put you in it." He replies in a grumpy tone.

I lean my head back and groan but get up knowing he's serious. I start to walk to the truck. I stop turning around, "Both of you stay here with Jay. I will be back by dinner and we will finish this discussion."

Taj walks up behind me, "Bring them or leave them, we are on a tight schedule. I am sure we could find something for them to do."

I move in front of the boys. Blocking his view of them, "Don't even think about it Taj, they are off limits."

He nods his head and walks to the truck. As he's walking, he grumbles; "You know, you having a suspended license is a pain in the ass."

I don't say anything, but follow him and jump into the passenger seat, he takes off as soon as my door closes.

Chapter 3

After a long day, Taj pulls up to the curb outside my place, it's dark outside. I get out and go to close the door but then notice both the cop car and uncle Phoenix's car.

"You've got to be kidding me." I groan.

Taj looks out the window. Once he sees it, he turns to me and sighs, "It's probably best if you leave your gun here with me. So if they toss you they won't find it."

I nod and pull it out and hand it to him. He puts it in his glove box and I close the passenger door. He signals and pulls off.

I walk up to the door to see just the boys, my Uncle Phoenix, cousin Charlie, his partner Roman; both who were still in their police uniforms, and my older brother Jack. Roman had been Charlie's partner for four years, so he knew us all pretty well. All of my roommates must be in their rooms or out of the house; none are big fans of cops.

I walk in tugging my sneakers off and putting them in the shoe basket next to the door. Jen had started this thing about not wearing shoes in the house, something about them tracking germs everywhere.

"Hey Kai, nice of you to join us." My brother Jack says sarcastically.

"Hey big bro, can I get you anything? Tea? Coffee?" I say with the same level of sarcasm.

"I must say, I'm a little disappointed you didn't call me the minute they showed up here." He adds.

"How did you know they were here? I know they didn't call you." I tell him.

Jack presses his lips into a thin line before answering, "Mika called me."

"Mika is five. He did not call you." I say shaking my head at him.

"Well I called looking for Sasha, his baseball coach called saying he hadn't shown up to his last four practices. I told Mika to take him the phone and he said that they'd been gone since Tuesday. Today is Thursday."

"Let me guess. You tracked their phones." I say, looking over at the boys.

"Yup." Jack says snarkily, obviously proud of himself that he finally put those computer skills to use.

Milos got angry, "You idiot! You were supposed to keep your phone off!" Then punched Sasha in the arm.

Sasha punched him in the arm back "I had to see if Stephanie texted me!"

"Don't be such a clueless potato! You've been friend zoned!" Milos yells at him.

Jack stopped them before they got in a fight, "Enough! You should both know better than to pull a stunt like this. I'm putting you on the next flight home." He states.

"Jack, how did you even get here from NYC so quickly?" I chimed in.

"The ticket receipt said California, LAX, I figured they'd be heading your way. Plus, I was only a day behind them." He says then looks at his watch.

Then suddenly, Charlie's partner, Roman, takes a few steps towards me and asks, "Do you want to tell us what you got rid of when you saw our patrol car?"

"Excuse me?" I say with attitude.

"You got out and handed the guy something before closing the door." He says.

"Sorry, don't know what you're talking about. I was saying thanks for the ride to my friend." I tell him.

"I've known you for three years. I doubt that." he says, narrowing his eyes at me.

I lift my shirt up mid stomach and do a slow turn to show him there is nothing in my waistband.

"What about your pockets?" Charlie asks.

I turn my pockets inside out and a large switchblade knife falls to the floor with a thud. *Ah crap,* I thought to myself, *I should have tossed that in Taj's glove box along with the gun! Well, too late now I guess.*

Uncle Phoenix picks it up, looks at it and looks at me, "The fuck you need this for?"

"Oh you know, opening packages." I say sarcastically.

"Don't be a smart ass." Uncle Phoenix warns.

"It's not illegal to have that is it detective? If it is you can talk to my lawyer. She's right upstairs... SARAH! CAN

YOU COME DOWN HERE…?" I scream towards the ceiling.

"No, you don't need a lawyer Kai." Uncle Phoenix says with a sigh rubbing his temples with his thumb and middle finger.

"NEVER MIND!" I yell towards upstairs.

Uncle Phoenix stops rubbing his temples and sighs "It's late, we will finish this later. Jack, they are your siblings. Now that they are no longer missing, it's not a police issue anymore. I'll leave them in your care, but please do keep me updated." He says, then walks out.

"Does that mean I can have my knife back?" I ask.

"Don't push your luck Kai." He warns over his shoulder as he walks out.

He walks out, as does Charlie and Roman. Jack sighs, obviously pretty pissed, "It is late, he says looking at his watch again. You two go to the guest bedroom, I'll sleep on the couch, and Kai you go to bed too, we will talk in the morning."

I got some sheets and blankets for Jack on the couch, then showed the boys to the guest bedroom. Sasha looks and says, "There's three beds in here, why is Jack sleeping on the couch?"

I start to walk out, but respond as they get changed, "He wants to make sure that we don't try to sneak out. He can see the front door and back door from where that couch is." He just has a 'oh' look on his face. I tell them goodnight and I head off down the hall. Once I get to my room, I send out a group text to my roommates that reads; 'cops are gone but Jack is sleeping on the couch'.

Jay was already asleep, so I got changed in the bathroom. I flipped the bathroom lights off after using the restroom and brushing my teeth. Walking out and over to our bed, I pull the sheets away and sit down. Swinging my legs and feet up, I put them underneath the covers.

Scooting down, and getting comfortable, I curl up next to him. I kiss the back of his head and he rolls over, pulling me closer to him and falls back to sleep. I smile and start to fall asleep.

Chapter 4

I woke up to yelling and breaking glass. I looked over and Jay had already left for work. I jumped out of bed, not having time to get dressed and walked out into the hall in Jay's t-shirt and underwear. I slowly walked down the hall. Milos and Sasha were in the doorway, half awake, with bed head. I walked up to their room, and Sasha gave out a 'what's going on' look, with the matching hand gesture. I shushed him before he said anything and pushed them into the guest room, closing the door behind me.

"I need both of you to stay here and be quiet," I whispered.

"Who's out there?" Milos asked.

"I'm going to find out but you need to stay here. Lock the door behind me and go sit in the bathroom." I handed them their phones.

I exited the guest room and waited until I heard the click of the door lock. I slowly walked toward and down the stairs. Peeking around the corner, I saw Jack with his back towards me, arguing with some guy that looked familiar, but I didn't quite recognize. Of course this happens when I don't have my gun and uncle Phoenix took my knife. Luckily they weren't in the kitchen. I tiptoed into the kitchen and grabbed one of the knives. If I learned one thing from the past, it's don't ever be unarmed or unable to protect yourself. I slid across the kitchen and pressed my back up against the wall, right next to the doorway that led to the living room. I listened to their argument. Jack was angry, he knew the guy in front of him but not the other one.

"I'm not here to argue with you Jack, I'm here to see Kai." says unknown #1.

"The fuck you are, Jake. Get back on your bike and go back to New York." Jack spits out.

"Not without talking to her first." Jake says.

"And why do you need to see her so bad?" Jack asks.

"She has something that belongs to Nick." Jake replies.

Nick? What would he be doing here? I thought to myself

That's when I hear a familiar voice. "Look man, I know you, as her brother, want to protect her, but I really need to see her."

"No way. Nick is it? I've heard of you, she left for a reason. Shit man, you put her in danger! Why would you come here knowing that?" Jack says assertively.

"The rest of my club don't know we are here, I promise." Nick says trying to sound convincing.

I step into the doorway. Jake and Nick look at me. Jack turns around but doesn't say anything. Now it was my turn to be angry.

"Nicki what the fuck are you doing here?" I say weakly.

He hates it when I call him that, so I use it on purpose, but he ignores it. He starts to step forward but stops when he sees the knife in my hand. "You don't need that. I'm not here to hurt you."

I just tighten my grip on the handle. "You need to leave."

"I'm not leaving until we talk. But first, you are going to put the knife down," Nick says, taking two steps forward.

I start to back up, "You stay away from me." Every step I take back, he steps forward.

"You forget how well I know you and how I am the one who trained you since the first day you walked into that MMA gym." He takes two more steps forward.

"Plus, on some level" he continues "you must still have some feelings left for me. Or were you just using me for sex?" Before I even blink, he rushes towards me and grabs my arm. I try to swing the knife at him but he expertly dodges it. He's bigger and stronger than me and all I manage to do is rip his jeans and slightly wound his leg. He knocks me over still holding my arm and tries to pin me to the ground.

"DROP THE KNIFE, KAI!" He screams.

"GET OFF OF ME!" I yell back.

I look over towards the living room and Jake and Jack are fighting, more like wrestling. I try to wiggle out from under him, but he just holds me down tighter, putting more of his weight on me. I yank my arm down and the knife slices his hand open. I take this opportunity to push my arm upward and hold the knife against his throat.

He stops and stares down at me. Leaning into it he smiles as it nicks his skin and he teases; "So on some level you do still love me. Or else you would have done it already."

"I have a new man now. You can't be here; danger follows you everywhere." I tell him, after blowing a strand of hair out of my face.

"Then do it. Push harder. Or are you trying to keep this part of your life from the people who live here?" He says leaning into it and staring me down at me with a wicked smile. I sigh, lowering the knife. He grabs it and throws it down the hallway. He smiles and looks at me but doesn't let me go.

"You look good, Kai." he says, flashing me that famous smile.

"Do you mind getting off of me?" I say annoyed.

"Can you behave?" he teases.

"Can you get the fuck off of me and out of my house?" I retort.

"Wrong answer, sweetheart." He says with a smirk.

I sigh and look at him for a moment then ask, "Why are you here?"

His smile fades and he brushes my long brownish black curly hair out of my face then leans over and whispers in my ear, "I'm here for my fucking kid. And don't lie. I can tell when you do." He says then leans back up.

"Like you would ever be a father." I throw in his face.

"That kid is part of my bloodline, he should be with his family." He says clearly trying to keep his cool.

"Why? So you can beat him all the time? Like your father used to beat you?" I spew out.

He slaps me across the face.

Flashback.

I woke up on a Saturday morning. I laid there, not liking the feeling in my stomach. I shot up, jumping out of bed and ran to the bathroom. I emptied the contents of my stomach into the toilet. I flushed it and sat on the floor in the bathroom leaning my head on the wall.

My sister Mira comes in and leans against the doorframe, "Sick again?"

This would make it the fifth morning in a row. She sighed handing me a grocery bag. It had ginger cookies, mouthwash and three pregnancy tests in it.

I look up at her and she gives me a weak smile, "Well we have to know for sure."

I took all three tests to make sure they were accurate; they take about 15 minutes. And all three were positive. I walked into my bedroom and slid down the wall.

"Of course they would find a way to have a lasting effect on me." I say with a sad laugh, a single tear slid down my cheek.

My sister sat down next to me, "Do you know who the father is?"

"Nick." I replied.

"Shit. Are you going to tell him?" She asks carefully.

"Fuck no." I look over at her and we both start to smile then start to laugh. She grabs my hand and interlaces her fingers into mine holding my hand in her lap.

"Well you have options," she says after a minute.

"Adoption is the only possible way this can end." I say after a moment.

"Are you sure? I have connections at the hospital I work at, but you need to be sure." She says with a serious look.

"I can't keep him or her, I'm only 19. I'm not ready to be a parent. And his or her father is dangerous. It's not safe for a baby to be in that position, his gang would treat it like their property, not as a person." I say, wiping away a tear.

"Okay. I will make a call." She says after a moment.

"No one can know about this, Mira." I say giving her a serious look.

She gets up and walks across the room grabbing her laptop, putting it on the bed and walks towards me as she says; "Which is why you are going on a six month vacation to London. Where you will deliver and some nice couple in England can adopt the baby and then you will come back like nothing happened."

"Why London?" I ask confused.

"If the baby is born in England, it will make it harder for Nick's gang to find him / her. But also, remember I spent fifteen months over there, doing that job I'm not supposed to talk about? Well that's where most of my contacts come from." She explains.

"Wait, I thought you said you didn't do much field work." I state, still a little confused.

"I didn't get much field work, they mostly used my computer hacking skills. Which is why it was harder to earn the contacts I have over there. And even now, years later they are still of some use. Trust me, this will be the best way to keep your baby out of Nick's hands." She says, then puts the tests in a small trash bag and takes them out to the bin.

End of flashback

Present day

I look at Nick, narrow my eyes at him, "I don't have them."

"Them?" Nick says confused.

Before Nick can say anything else, I hear a click of a gun being cocked. I look up and it's Taj, Ty and Jade from my club. Taj had a gun to Nick's head.

"If you want to keep breathing, I suggest you get off of her." Taj warns.

"Take it easy, man. I'm getting up." Nick says, as he puts his hands in the air. Blood from his wound starts to flow down his arm in streams.

"Slowly." Taj warns.

As soon as he gets off of me, Jade walks over helping me up. Looking me up and down, she smirks and asks "What happened to your pants, hot stuff?"

I look down and look back up, "Didn't have time to get dressed".

Ty throws Nick a hand towel and he puts pressure to stop the bleeding.

Nick looks confused and angry. Looking around them he spews out, "What do you mean you don't have *them*?" Putting an emphasis on *'them'*.

"Exactly what I said." I say calmly.

"Where are they?" He asks with a pissed off tone with a hint of possessiveness.

"Somewhere in the adoption system. Or with their new family."

"YOU CAN'T DO THAT WITHOUT MY PERMISSION!" Nick screams at me.

"All I had to say was I was nineteen and the father was a violent criminal and they had no problem taking them." I said, trying to keep my composure.

Taj finally speaks up, "Sounds like she doesn't have what you came for and it's time for you to leave."

Nick brushes a shaking hand through his black hair and walks out the door. But he stops just outside the door, turns and says; "This isn't over, I will be back."

Taj and Ty step into his view path of me. "Not advisable for your health," Ty says.

Then they both stand as straight as they can, "Plus we will be here." Taj adds. And with that, Nick leaves.

Chapter 5

Jade walks down the hall grabbing the knife, it has Nick's blood on it. She puts it in a Ziploc bag and uses a paper towel to wipe up any blood smeared on the wood floor, then puts the paper towel in the bag too. "I'll get rid of it." She says while putting it in her purse.

I go over to the cabinet and grab the broom and dustpan to clean up some broken plates. They had gotten knocked off the island counter and shattered on the floor. While I was cleaning up the plates, Jade went upstairs to get me some pants and to check on the boys.

"The boys want the secret password before opening the door for me." She says as she comes back, then hands me a pair of sweats.

"Salted watermelon." I tell her.

"Really?" She gives me a weird look.

"They came up with it when they were like seven and stuck with it." She walked back down the hall and up the stairs.

I put on the sweats and start pacing around the living room, "Who does he think he is just walking in here like that? After what he did!"

"Why don't you sit down? You're not going to solve anything by walking back and forth like that. Sit." Ty says as he steps in front of me stopping me from pacing.

"Wait, what happened to Jack?" I suddenly realized.

"We caught him wrestling in the yard with some guy. We broke it up and told them to both walk it off." Taj tells me.

"Thanks. How did you know to come here?" I ask.

Jade walks in with the boys, "You left your phone in the guest room with the boys. I was on your emergency contact list. Milos and Sasha called me."

"There was a lot of yelling and all your roommates had already left. We thought you could use some help." Sasha says thinking they were in trouble.

"You guys were great. It was a big help that you called Jade." I told them as I got up and walked over to them and pulled them into a hug. They both smiled at each other. I continue; "Now that you are up, why don't you get some cereal? Jack will be back to take you to the airport." They both nod their heads and walk into the kitchen.

Jack comes back in, putting his iPhone in his pocket as he walks up. His shirt is torn, hair messed up and his lip is split on the right corner. He pulls out a chair from the kitchen table and sits down, out of breath still. He looks at the boys for a moment, then says; "Now that you two have had something to eat, why don't you upstairs and brush your teeth. When you are done, grab your bags and bring them downstairs. A cab will be here in twenty minutes to take us to the airport."

The boys get up, put their bowls in the sink, and then walk upstairs. I sit down in a chair next to Jack. He doesn't say anything for a while. He just stares out the back slider.

"Have you talked to Caiden at all? It's been a few months since he moved here." Jack asks after a moment.

"No. We haven't talked since I helped him move into his new condo. I texted him to invite him over for a beer, but he never responded." I reply.

Caiden may be my brother, but he was a traitor as far as I was concerned, becoming a Raven and all. But at least he isn't a snitch, that would be worse.

Taj walks over changing the subject, "Get dressed and let's go. Not telling the others is not an option, Kai." I get up and walk towards the stairs, squeezing Jack's shoulder as I walk behind him.

Chapter 6

I tossed and turned in the bed in the spare room at the club. Some of the younger members were told to stay at the club for the night during the meeting. It was ten at night and I snuck out with Jessie and Luca. Two guys who were a year younger and the other a couple months older than me from the club. We all need this to let off some steam, so we went to the closest party we could find. We took a taxi so we wouldn't have to find parking, but also so no one would be tempted to drink and drive.

The party was so huge it took up three houses. We said we would meet back up around two in the morning. I went into the middle house first, I figured I would start out slow and just have a couple beers. But, several beers and shots later, I was pretty drunk. I walked up some stairs and just barely made it to the top. I saw a sofa and a bar on the second floor. I got another beer and then went to sit on the sofa. There were lots of people dancing and grinding in one corner, then in another corner people were making out.

I was on the sofa in the middle of the room, when two guys walked over and sat on either side of me. The one on the left leans his head on my shoulder, while the other puts his hand on my leg. I look at him and raise an eyebrow at him, he laughs and leans over towards my ear so I can hear him over the music.

"You here alone darlin'?" He tries to talk over the music.

"So what if I am?" I respond.

"Ahh where's your man? Can't be very smart to leave you by yourself at a party."

"He's at work." I say taking another long swig from my beer.

"At this time of night?" he drawls.

"He's covering a coworkers shift. And besides, I doubt you came over here to talk about my boyfriend." I tell him.

"You would be correct darlin'. Can I get you another beer?" He offers as he extends out his hand.

"Sure, I'll take another beer." I finished my current beer in two long swigs.

"Is your friend okay?" I look over at his friend who still has his head on my shoulder. He ignores my question as he grabs my now empty bottle and walks away to get more beer. The guy walks back over and hands me another beer.

"So do you got a name? Or just call people darlin' and give them beer?" I yell over the pulsing music.

He laughs reaching over and pushing his friend off of me and onto the empty sofa seat. Leaning back, he smiles, "Daren." He says sticking out his hand. I shake his hand while telling him my name. I'm about halfway through the beer he got me and he offers to get me another.

I laugh, "Well Daren, if I didn't know better, I'd say you are trying to get me drunker."

He laughs, "Is that even a word?"

I just shrug my shoulders. "Another beer it is then!" he says with a laugh.

Then out of nowhere, someone yanks my beer out of my hand while saying, "She's not gonna need it."

I look up to see four guys from the club standing in front of me. They're a little blurry but I blink my eyes a couple times to focus. Zach is standing to my left, while Will is standing in front of me. I look around him and Alex is holding a drunk Jessie by the collar of his shirt.

Will looks pissed, "Seriously Kai? With everything that's going on right now, you sneak out to go to a party?" He doesn't give me time to answer. He grabs both sides of my jacket and pulls me up. I stumble a little and almost fall but he still has a hold of my jacket. Bunching the jacket into one hand, he drags me towards the stairs.

"If you think...we are...going down those stairs..." I mumble as we continue walking. I don't even finish my mumbled sentence. He stops, turns around, bends over and picks me up by the waist and throws me over his shoulder then walks towards the stairs. I didn't have much time to react, I just tried to hold on and wrap my arms around him in an upside-down fashion. He starts to walk down the stairs and gets lots of hoots, whistles, and cheering from the crowd around us. They probably think he's about to get some or something. He gets to the bottom of the stairs, but he doesn't put me down. He walks all the way to the car before putting me back on my own feet. I had to resist the urge to puke, but after a moment, I was good and he motioned for me to get in the car.

"Oh come on, it's not even three in the morning yet, you don't want to party at all?" I say joking. Will steps closer to me with his hand clenched on the back collar of my shirt.

"Get in the car, Kai." He says with a threatening tone.

15 minutes later

We are driving and I see a waffle place. "WAFFLES!" I yell.

"No waffles for you," says a tired Zach from the passenger seat.

"You sir are not the king of waffles. I say put it to a vote." I announce.

"We are not voting on this." Zach says.

Jessie, Luca and I all start chanting 'Waffles" starting out low, "Waffles" a little louder, "Waffles!" we yell the last one.

Zach and Will look at each other and Will says, "Fine you can have waffles but we are going to the drive through and we have to wait till we get to the club to eat them." We pull up to the drive through window and try to place our order. We roll down the back window and the other two crowd the window.

"Guys one at a time." I yell at them.

We all try to order at the same time. Jessie punches Luca in the shoulder, "Hey man you better back off, ladies first."

"Hey man," Luca fires back "you better watch yourself. I will kick your ass."

I push both of them off of the seat and go to order. But before I can order they pull me back away from the window.

The cashier doesn't know what to do. Even though they are open 24 hours a day, they probably don't get too many customers at this time of night.

Will rolls up the back window and orders our food. Zach turns around in his seat and yells at us, "Seriously guys get back in your seats and pull your seatbelts on. Don't make me come back there."

Chapter 7

I woke up with a huge hangover. I sit up and realize the club was a disaster. Furniture fallen over, a hole in the lampshade, a soda bottle had fallen over and was still dripping soda off the side of the counter, and a bra was swinging from the ceiling fan. Ok, I still have my bra on, so that's not mine. I look over to see Luca and Jessie still asleep, both with their jackets under their heads and pieces of waffles everywhere half eaten. Jessie had a piece in his hair. I remember we had a food fight, but where are my shoes? I look around to find we are the only ones in the club bar. I kick Jessie's feet. He stirs but doesn't wake up. I scoot closer to him and jab him in the ribs with my foot.

"What the…" he shoots up with his fist raised until he realizes it's me. He nods at me and looks over at Luca smacking him in the back of the head, "Wake up, asshole."

"Oww what was that for?" He grumbles then rolls off his side and onto his back.

"I don't remember much of the lecture we got last night. How much trouble were we in?" I ask.

"A shit ton. We snuck out after we were specifically told not to leave club grounds." Jessie replies. It was quiet for a moment after that.

I broke the silence saying, "I don't know man, but I got a headache right now."

"You know what the best cure for a hangover is?" Jessie asks with a smile.

"More booze?" Luca says.

"Exactly. We might as well take something to take the edge off." He says with a smile.

I stand up and brush my legs off. As the boys stand up, I pull a hair tie off my wrist, throwing my hair up into a high bun.

47

We walk over to the bar and look at what is in stock. "Score!" They both say as I hold up a bottle of vodka in my hand. We start taking shots and laughing at each other's jokes. We then fill three water bottles up with Vodka. We walk out the door and as we are walking down the stairs, the alarms start to blare, going off.

"Ah shit! They must have armed the alarm before they left, to screw with us" I yell over the alarm. We all cover our ears and walk out of the stairwell. I walk into the kitchen and enter the alarm code; it halts to a stop.

We lock the back door as we go out and start to walk off. We get out of the parking lot and are walking down the sidewalk, when a cop car rolls by and flips a U-turn. He slowly rolls behind us.

"Luca, do you still have that warrant?" I ask, but don't look at him.

"Ya, I haven't paid the fines yet." He says quietly, not looking over at me.

"Shit. Should one of us be the rabbit, or do you want to stay together?" I ask.

"Together, make a run for the alley. Their car can't follow that way." Jessie replies.

"You guys ready?" They both nod their heads. "Three. Two. One!" We take off running as fast as we can towards the alley, their sirens wail behind us. We run into a neighborhood jumping several fences. We would have been faster if we weren't a little tipsy from the shots. But Jessie was right, my headache was gone. I put my arms out stopping them. "What?!" They both ask out of breath.

"Your phones, stash them in the alley way when we go through. We can't have our phones on us, they can track them" I tell them.

They both nod and we continue running. We get to an alley and stash our phones behind a dumpster. We take a break for a minute to catch our breath and Luca pukes in the bushes.

49

"My friend Kat lives two streets over; she will hide us there." I tell them.

"Lead the way. Lu, you good?" Jessie asks and Luca walks over to us wiping his mouth with the back of his left hand.

"Good to go." Luca replies.

And with that we continue running until we get to Kat's place. I pound on the door and get a, "alright, I'm coming you gotta give me a second to get to and open the door."

She flings the door open and is confused when she sees me.

"We need you to hide us!" She waves us in and we rush in explaining a little bit of what was happening.

"I leave for a two week trip to Spain with Diego on Thursday. You can stay till then." She says with a hint of being hesitant.

"You are amazing," I tell her as I hug her. We sit on the couch, make introductions and catch up.

Chapter 8

After a couple of days of staying in Kat's apartment, Luca and I went out to get some supplies. Jessie had gone home at this point, but I would feel weird leaving Luca at Kat's place by himself. He couldn't go to his place yet, that's the first place the cops will look for him and he couldn't afford to pay the fines till the end of the month.

I went to buy some alcohol and Luca bought some groceries. We pretty much emptied Kat's fridge and cabinets. We get back to the apartment and Kat and Luca start whispering to each other. I give them a look and Luca smiles then holds up a bag of brownies. They look at each other and laugh. "They are special brownies," Luca reports.

"Where did you even get those?" I ask.

"I ran into this guy I went to high school with, while we were at the store. He was always known to have some on him. I asked as a joke and he said I could have some at a discount." Luca explains.

"Well I'm good, I'll just drink some beers." I say as I finish helping Kat put the groceries away.

An hour and a half later, Luca and Kat were pretty stoned. Diego and I only had a few beers and a little from an old bottle of vodka Kat had. So I wasn't too drunk, maybe just buzzed.

"Kat did you get a hold of Jay?" I ask.

"Ya...he said he would see you on Thursday. And that he would let Jade know you guys were here." She replied.

We watched some news on the tv and talked about some of the reporter's outfits. Kat said she could be the main female anchors stylist and make her look way better than her current stylist.

Then all of a sudden, Kat's apartment door got kicked in. I jumped up, running to Kat's room. There was a lot of swearing and yelling behind me, but I just kept going. I bust through the door and dove towards her bed to get my gun out of my bag from under her bed. Grabbing the bag, I dropped to my knees and turned the bag upright. I unzipped the front and started to pull stuff out. I saw it at the bottom of the bag and almost grabbed it, when someone's big arms wrapped around me and pulled me backwards. He had one arm around my stomach with my back pressed into his chest. The other hand was wrapped around my wrist holding it against my chest. I struggled to get out of his grip. He let go of my wrist, then moved one arm to wrap over my chest and grabbed onto my shoulder to get a better grip. I looked down at his arm and see his gang tattoo, it's a bunch of ravens flying out of a tree. The base of the tree starts at his wrist, with roots extending out onto his hand. Shit, we must have crossed onto the Ravens territory. When Luca bought that bag of brownies with his

Wolves vest on, they got word we were visiting and a scout must have followed him back to the apartment. We had been having territorial disputes with them lately. We struggle some more but he is stronger than me. He pushes me onto the bed on my stomach, putting his weight on top of me. Struggling to get my hands behind my back and into zip ties, he lets go of my left arm and focuses on my right arm. I use this opportunity to elbow him across the left side of his jaw. This catches him off guard and he falls off me. I dive for my bag and grab my gun. I pull it out then roll over as I pull the slide back and it clicks. I point it at him and he freezes.

We stare at each other for a moment, then from the other room we hear more yelling and gunshots. The Raven member slowly walks over to the windowsill and puts one leg through, straddling the windowsill. He looks at me for a moment, smiles and jumps out of Kats bedroom window onto the fire escape and escapes. I lower my gun, letting it fall against the floor with a thud, but keep it in my hand. I lean my head back against the floor staring at the spinning ceiling fan for a moment. I hear someone walk through the doorway and I lean back up and raise my gun at the figure.

"Woah! Easy tiger." Will says, putting his hands up in the air.

I lower the gun again and let my head fall back against the floor, as I try to catch my breath. Will walks over and takes my gun out of my hand, putting it back in my backpack after he unloads it.

"Come on, we have to get out of here." He says extending out a hand to help me up. I grab his hand and he lifts me up.

We walk out of the bedroom, then through the living room and three Raven members were on their knees, with their hands tied behind their backs. One had a towel tied around his bleeding leg; he must have been hit with a bullet. A fourth Raven member was laying on his back on the floor with a fifth Raven member holding pressure to the fourth member's abdomen, which was soaked through the towel with blood.

"Will is going to get you home, we will deal with this." Zach tells me.

As we walk out, I apologize to Diego about the door and the mess, then we walk out of Kats apartment. On the street, I get into Will's black Mercedes and pull on my seat belt. He gets into the driver's seat, but before he pulls out, he reaches in the back seat and grabs a bag. "That was quite a bit of action and blood. If you need to puke, puke in the bag." He says, handing it to me.

"I think I'm good." I say not looking at him and staring out the window. He puts the bag in my lap and with that said, he pulls out and we drive towards my house.

Chapter 9

Will pulls onto our street and parks under a street light. He puts it in park, turns the car off and we both get out. As we walk up the front steps, we say nothing and a distant echo of a train horn can be heard.

I walk into the house and get a, "Hey look who came back. We were about to file a missing persons report on you." They all say jokingly.

They all knew where I was, Kat was a mutual friend of all of us. However, they don't know about my 'work' life. So Zach is going to have to debrief Kat and Diego about the incident and explain to them not to talk to anyone about the run-in with the Ravens.

They all stop talking when Will walks through the door. He nods to them and walks towards the hallway, "You should get some rest." He says quietly as he walks by. I walk not protesting that it was only noon, he walks behind me as we go up the stairs. He watches me take off my shoes, bra and jeans. I walk into the bathroom and grab a sleeping shirt, slipping it on after I take my shirt off. I walk back into the bedroom and get into bed.

"I will see you tomorrow. Your security detail will be here in an hour."

"My security detail?" I question as I turn onto my side and look at him.

"Sean and Nate are going to make sure you don't have any more hostile visitors. They'll be here a few days."

"So, they are coming to sit in their car across the street to watch me?" I ask.

"You know the timing was amazing today right? If we hadn't shown up at Kat's when we did, it would have ended very differently." He says with a sigh, then walks out without another word.

Chapter 10

I wake up and look at my clock, it's around 11pm. My stomach starts to growl. I go downstairs then into the kitchen and grab a snack. I eat some leftover pizza and make some popcorn. My roommate Collin is up watching tv. I sit down next to him and hand him his own bowl of popcorn. We were watching tv for about an hour and someone knocked on the door.

Collin opens the door and I hear, "Why are you here Natasha? You and I both know all you are going to do is start some shit."

"I'm just here to see Dawson about the divorce papers." She says sweetly.

"That's what lawyers are for." He tells her. She brushes past him while patting him on the cheek. Her smile fades when she sees me.

I roll my eyes and yell, "Dawson you've got a visitor."

I get up to leave but she grabs my left wrist and says, "Don't roll your eyes at me bitch." I look down at her hand and back up.

"You better be very fucking careful what you do next," I say while my right hand balls into a fist.

Dawson may let her get away with a lot, but with the history we have, she's on thin ice. Collin doesn't know what to do and just stands by the still open door watching us. She smiles and lets go of my wrist only to haul off and slap me across the face, sending buzzing stings across the left side of my face, splitting my bottom lip.

I wasn't about to let her get away with that. I threw a hard right hook and hit her right across her cheek and she went down hard. She gets up then crashes into me and we land on the wood coffee table and break some vases that were on the table. I get a sharp pain, followed by a dull ache from my ribs. I push her off the table and get up. She

gets back up but before she can recover, I backhand slap
her and grab her by the hair and her jacket and throw her
over the couch. I jump over the couch and land next to her.
She gets up and swings, hitting me in the cheek. She goes
to punch me again but I block her with my left arm and
punch her with my right. She goes down again. I stand
over her, bending down and grabbing her shirt, lifting her
up. I punch her with my right hand and as I do let go of her
shirt. I do it again. I rear back to do it a third time but
someone hooks their arm around mine and grabs the back
of my shirt pulling me back and off of her. He throws me
against the wall and holds me there with an arm across my
chest

"RELAX! IT'S OVER!" Sean yells at me.

"LET ME GO!" I shout as I push against him.

"RELAX!" He repeats as he pushes me back against
the wall.

I push against him again and he pushes me towards the door holding onto the back collar of my shirt, "Let's walk it off!"

He asks Collin to hand him a dish towel to wrap around my now bloody knuckles. He pushes me out the door.

"Walk!" He orders.

"She started it!" I protest.

"Well I'm ending it. Now walk!" He pushes me forward.

Chapter 11

We went back to the house about two and a half hours later. Melody, my nurse roommate, Dawson, and Collin, were cleaning up some broken glass. While Dakota and Julian were sitting on the couch watching. Julian is another one of my roommates.

"And in walks our champion of the night!" Julian says as he starts to clap

"You beat Tasha's ass!" Dakota pipes in.

Sean follows me in and stands in the corner. I turn towards Dawson, "Look Dawson, I know she was your ex and it was your fight."

He cuts me off, "She slapped you. She should have known better. I'm proud of you for beatin her ass. We're good." He says with a wink.

"In the kitchen, sit on the table. I'm gonna look you over." Melody says as she walks over.

"Mel I'm fine." I say with a straight face and a reassuring smile, trying to sound convincing.

"In the kitchen, sit on the table." She repeats a little more seriously.

I walk over to the kitchen and sit down. She grabs her first aid kit from under the counter. I tease her, "Our own private nurse to the rescue."

She looks me over, "The laceration on your cheek doesn't need stitches nor the one on your eyebrow. Your split lip will also heal on its own." She looks at my right hand unwrapping the dish towel. "These cuts and abrasions on your knuckles will heal on their own. But you should ice them." She puts a bandage over my knuckles.

"Thanks nurse Melody." I tease her.

I jump down and she bumps into my side and I take in a sharp breath.

"You okay?" She asks.

"Ya fine just sore." I reply

I go sit back on the couch. Collin walks in. He had been watching us. He watches me wince a little when I sit down. "Lift up your shirt Kai. I want to see your side."

"In case you didn't know Collin, I have a boyfriend." I joked.

"You should check her ribs Mel, they went down hard on the side of that coffee table." He says turning towards her.

"She doesn't need to, I'm fine," I give him a look.

Melody walks back over lifting up my shirt. We see a large bruise starting to form. "We need to get you to a hospital."

"Not necessary." I say as I shake my head.

"We need to get your ribs x-rayed to see if they are broken. If they are broken, they could puncture something." Melody reports.

"It's just a bruise." I reply.

Sean speaks up, "My buddy Tango was a medic when he was in the military. He mainly just helps out friends and freelances now, I'll call him."

"It's four in the morning. Again, not necessary." I say but he ignores me and calls him. Tango gets to our place around 5:30 am.

"So, I understand we have an unwilling patient." He says as he walks through the door.

"Hey Tango man!" Sean yells out in a greeting.

They bro hug and Sean tells him a little about what's going on. I sneak out of the room and sneak up stairs and go into my room. I put my phone on a charger and the door opens. I look and it's doc Tango and Sean.

"Did you think you could sneak out and get away so easily?" Sean asks.

"I told you I'm fine." I say as I put my phone on the nightstand.

Tango spoke, breaking the tension, "Well, let's just make sure of that shall we? I hear you were in quite the tussle. Sean, you can wait out in the hall."

"I should probably stay." He starts to say but Tango cuts him off.

"If I can handle injured soldiers. I'm pretty sure I can handle a twenty something year old."

Sean nods walking out and shuts the door behind him.

Tango turns towards me, "Alright take off your shirt and lay on the bed."

"Jeez doc, at least buy me dinner first." I joke.

He smiles but doesn't move. I take off my shirt, leaving my bra on. And lay on my bed. He rechecks all the stuff Melody did, then moves to my ribs. He starts to poke and feel them and I shoot up.

"Shit man, what are you trying to do?!"

"I know they hurt, but I need to see if they are broken." He says and I lay back down and he continued his inspection.

He talks while he looks at my ribs. "That's a pretty interesting scar you got on your left shoulder there. When were you shot? Through and through I see."

"A little more than a year ago." I say looking away.

"Did you need to do physical therapy?" He asks.

"No, it healed just fine without physical therapy." I say with an annoyed tone.

"You know that ignoring it is not good. You need to deal with it."

"So you're a psychiatrist and physical therapist now too?" I say sarcastically.

"No, but I know a lot about trauma. It needs to be dealt with in a healthy way. Not ignored."

I change the subject, "So what's the prognosis for the ribs doc?" I say sitting up on my elbows and looking at him.

He sighs. Looks at me for a second then replies, "Mostly just bruised, a couple probably fractured but none broken. They should heal in about six weeks."

"Perfect." I say as I sit up putting my shirt back on.

"Does anyone know about it?" He says nodding to my shoulder.

"Only like five or six people. So don't go blabbing to anyone." I tell him.

"Doctor patient confidentiality. But I need to tell them about your ribs and special instructions." He says trying to pull off a reassuring smile.

"Fine." I say standing up and walking towards the door.

We walk downstairs and he tells everyone that was home about my bruised and fractured ribs that were on my left side. I look over to the window bench and see a very concerned Jay.

Tango continues, "I will be back in a couple days to check on you. Everyone be careful. No bumping into her too hard and no roughhousing. She can't do any heavy lifting and no running or jogging just to be safe. Got it?" Everyone nodded their heads.

With that he leaves and everyone gets up to go to bed.

Jay walks over to Collin, "Where the fuck were you? Just standing there? Like a little bitch? Why didn't you stop them?" He was yelling at Collin.

I go to calm Jay down but Julian stops me, "I got it".

He is very mature for an eighteen year old. He pulls Jay away from Collin and comforts a scared Collin.

Jay walks over to me gently putting his arm around me. "Let's go to bed."

I give an apologetic look towards Collin and he nods. Jay and I then walk off to get some sleep. Sean was going to call the club and push the meeting a couple days. We went slowly up the stairs. And when we got to our room I got into an oversized shirt and underwear then went to get in bed. I slowly slid into bed and under the covers. Jay asked if I needed anything then got into bed next to me careful to not bump me.

"Let's get some sleep," He says after kissing me on the lips then the forehead and we settled in.

Chapter 12

A few days later, my ribs were still fairly painful. I woke up needing to pee and get some water. I look at the clock and it's around 7:30 am. I slowly got out of bed so I wouldn't wake up Jay. Walking across the room, I slightly crack the curtains and look outside and it's gloomy and rainy. I walk out of my room and down the hall to the bathroom. The tile floor is cold on my warm feet and I leap onto the warm blue shag floor mat. After using the restroom and drinking some water I turn off the light, open the door and walk out. I start to walk back to my room and hear a weird noise down stairs.

I slide and slowly but quietly walk along the wall, stopping just next to the top of the stairs and think I hear unfamiliar voices. I walk back to my room and slide on some jeans with a belt, then grab my gun, my taser and a flashlight out of the night stand drawer. One of my roommates, Teo, also keeps a similar set up. I walk in his room without knocking. He raises his head looking at me.

"I have a feeling something isn't right downstairs." I whisper.

He sits up looking down at my taser on my hip, gun and flashlight in hand, he gets up and grabs his own set up.

He walks over to me and says, "I got your back."

We walk silently down the hall and down the stairs. I get to the bottom of the stairs and Dakota is laying on the ground next to the door. I look back at Teo and point at Dakota he nods and checks on him. I round a corner and go into the kitchen. Melody is on the floor with a knife in her stomach struggling to breathe.

"Teo! In here." I call out.

"Oh fuck!" He says as he runs in and stops.

We hear a noise outside. Teo puts his taser and flashlight on the counter and his gun in the back of his waistband.

"Go! I got this." He says kneeling down next to her.

I nod and walk to the back door. I push the panic button on the security alarm and it goes off. I open the door and two guys are holding a bloody Dawson back. I look down and two guys are beating the crap out of Collin. One takes a knife out of his pocket and I raise my gun pointing it at the pond and let out a shot. They all jump, turn to look at me and freeze where they are. Aiming it higher, I point it at the guy with a knife. He puts his hands up and drops the knife. Collin groans and rolls over. I hear sirens getting closer and closer. I put my gun in the back of my waistband.

Two cop cars pull up. "ON YOUR KNEES! LET ME SEE YOUR HANDS!"

We all drop to our knees and put our hands on the back of our heads. One of them looks over at Collin and radios for a medic. The other cop orders us to separate. "I WANT

EVERYONE WHO LIVES HERE ON THE RIGHT AND
THOSE WHO DON'T ON THE LEFT!"

"Officer two others are injured inside, one very
badly." I inform him. He radios for additional medics.
Another cop car pulls up and the intruders are all put in
handcuffs first, there are five of them. Just then my cousin
and Roman pull up in their patrol car. Roman looks around
and asks the first responding cops, "Did you search them?"

"Only the offenders, not the residents. But we got an
eye on them." He reports.

"Are you armed Kai?" Roman asks as he walks over.

"Yep." I respond.

"Don't move. Where is it?" He asks.

"Back of my waistband." I tell him.

He walks around and I keep my hands on the back of my
head. He grabs my gun and cuffs me walking over and
sitting me down on the porch.

I hear one of the cops saying, "There was a huge wreck up the road. Paramedics are twenty minutes out."

"The girl in the kitchen won't last that long. She's losing too much blood." the other whispers.

"Cuz, Roman, let me help her please." I ask them.

"What are you going to do?" Charlie asks.

"I'll figure it out. But it's better than doing nothing." I tell them.

They nod and uncuff me. I run in, stopping in the kitchen doorway, "Ohh fuck."

Teo had his hands on her wound around the knife.

He looks back at me, "What do we do?"

I stare at her in shock for a moment. There was a lot of blood. It was pooling around her and a little was coming out of her mouth. While Teo was looking at me, in panic she reached down and pulled it out. Not good, blood started to squirt out. She should know better since she is a nurse. I snapped out of it.

"Pressure! More pressure!" I yell.

Walking over to her, I look her over. She is bleeding from her stomach, mouth and leg.

I look up at one of the cops, "You! I need a belt! There should be one in the laundry room down the hall. The one with a poster on the door." I tell him.

"We can be more efficient; I have a tourniquet in my car." He says then runs off down the hall and out the door.

I push my hands down over Teo's. I look at one of my roommates Riley who is standing in the corner.

"Riley, go upstairs to the hallway walk in closet. On the top shelf towards the back there is a box labeled 'Emergencies only' grab it bring it here."

He nods and runs off.

The cop comes back with the tourniquet, "Keep pressure miss. I know first aid."

The cop talks as he works "I'm going to wrap this around her leg and tighten it as much as I can. She's going to scream but I need to tighten it to stop the bleeding."

I lean over so Melody can see my face, "Mel I'm sorry but this is going to hurt."

She nods. I lean back and nod at the cop. He starts to tighten it and she starts to scream but only a gurgled groan comes out with a blob of blood being coughed out. I check her pulse and Riley comes running with the box.

"Open it and take out the blue folder. Look where it has Melody's information. Did you find it?" I ask.

He nods.

"Good now look at all our roommates' info, who has the same blood type as her?"

He looks through the papers, "Sam, Sam is outside".

"SAM WE NEED YOU!" I yell.

Sam comes running in and he starts to freak out seeing all the blood.

"Sam! Sam focus on me." He looks at me. "She's losing a lot of blood. You are the only one in the house who has the same blood type as her."

He doesn't hesitate, "What do I need to do?" He asks.

"Roll up your sleeve." I motion for him to get on his knees and whisper in his ear, "It's none of my business but I have to ask before we do this. Do you have any conditions or diseases?" I lean back with an apologetic look.

"It's ok, I understand. And no, I don't." He tells me.

Jay steps in, "I got it. Where's the med kit?" I jerk my head towards the box.

He gets it out and pulls out an IV. Jay ties a plastic rope around Sam's arm and finds a vein and then does the same with Melody. He starts the transfusion, untying the rope from melody's arm and he checks her pulse.

"It's getting stronger." He reports.

Just then four paramedics run in taking over. Another two are out in the yard helping Collin. I go to clean my hands off. I get the excess blood off, but there is a red tint to my hands.

I walk outside to go check on Collin. As I walk by the intruders, the one who had the knife smiles and says, "Ah! There you are. We've been looking for you. Too bad we had to party without you."

"The fuck did you just say?" I say as I stop and turn around.

He says something in Russian and it clicks, Natasha's old boyfriend has ties with a Russian gang.

"You piece of shit!" I punch him across the face but before I can get another in Charlie and Roman grab me and throw me against a cop car putting me back in cuffs. I let out a quiet groan, well that hurt.

Jay yells, "Careful she has fractured ribs!"

Roman turns me around so my back and cuffed hands are against the car. Charlie pulls my shirt up. The bruises had gotten larger.

"How the fuck did this happen?! And please tell me you went to the hospital to get this checked out." Charlie asks.

"Well not exactly." I say.

"What do you mean not exactly?" Roman asks.

"We had a guy who was a medic when he was in the military come look at it."

Roman shakes his head, "Screw that, you are going to a hospital." He pulls me off the cop car and drags me to their car putting me in the back seat. They drive off with me in cuffs.

Chapter 13

We pull into the crowded parking lot, find a spot and we get out. Charlie helps me get out, putting his hand on the back of my head so I don't hit it as I get out. We get lots of stares from people as we walk into the emergency room.

"Hey Officers, what can I do for you?" A nurse asks. Charlie steps forward while Roman still has a hold of my arm.

"This is my cousin Kai. We need to get her checked out. Specifically, her ribs. They are badly bruised, potentially fractured or broken."

The nurse nods and leads us to a room. Roman lets go of my arm and points towards the bed, "Sit". We wait about twenty minutes and then a doctor walks in.

"My name is Doctor Mason. And you must be Kai." The doctor announces as he walks in.

"Sup." I say with a nod.

"You'll need to uncuff her officer." The doctor says to Roman.

Roman walks over and uncuffs me raising his eyebrows at me, "Behave yourself."

The doc walks over to me, "So the nurse said you have some bruised ribs. Potentially broken." He lifts up my shirt. "That's quite the bruise you've got there. We'll need to do some X-rays."

"I'd rather not. You know too much radiation and shit." I say.

"Kai!" Charlie says, "Don't be rude."

"Okay mom." I tease.

He rolls his eyes.

The doc continues, "The radiation is minimal. We will get you to radiology in half an hour to forty-five minutes. Wait here."

And with that he leaves. Roman and Charlie have to go back to the station and fill out paperwork. They inform me I am not being charged with anything, but I better get the X-ray and do what the doctor says.

I was playing a game on my phone and I heard a commotion down the hall. I get up to see what it is and there's nurses running in.

"24 year old male. Combative. Multiple track marks on his arms. Laceration on the side of his head. Sir we are not trying to hurt you! You need to calm down!" A nurse says trying to get control over the situation.

"Get off me you fuckin bitch." The patient yells.

Why does that voice sound familiar? I think to myself. I walk into the side of the doorway to see what's happening. He lays his shoulder into one nurse knocking her over.

"Get off me!" the patient yells again.

The gap gives me a clear shot and I am stunned. He continues to fight them as they struggle to put him in restraints. I walk in quickly.

"Ma'am you can't be in here!" Another nurse yells.

I ignore her and walk up to him. I put a hand on his chest, "LOUIE STOP!"

He stops moving and just stares at me. The nurses scramble taking this opportunity to put him in restraints.

"Kai?" He says surprised and out of breath.

Chapter 14

The nurses leave the room after taping gauze to his wound. I pull the chair away from the wall and next to his bed so we can talk.

"Kai what are you doing here?" Louie asks.

"Waiting for X-rays." I lift up the side of my shirt and show him the bruises.

"Dang! Who kicked your ass?" He says jokingly.

"She got in a single good tackle. But she paid for it." I say in a tough tone.

"That's the Kai I know. Don't take shit from nobody. I have to say I've missed you. It's been what six, seven months?" He says as he thinks about it for a moment.

"No, has it really been that long?" I ask.

"I don't know. Like I said I miss you but you had to get away from Isaac. That was a bad relationship. He used to leave you covered in bruises." He says after a moment.

I nod but don't say anything for a minute.

"It was a bad relationship and that is why I broke up with him. You need to get away from him but for a different reason." I say pointing to the needle tracks on his arm.

"You think I don't know that Kai?" He says.

A few minutes later his phone buzzes and I grab it off the bedside table.

"I can't believe you still have a flip phone Louie." I say sitting back down.

"Those smartphones they sell are being watched by the man. They have more technology to spy on us now than before." He says with a serious look.

I laugh, "You were paranoid before the drugs. I'm sure they aren't helping you now." I tell him and he smiles.

I flip open his phone and read the text. I scramble out of the chair next to Louie's bed. I toss the phone onto the bed. And walk quickly towards the door.

"What's wrong?" He asks.

"Isaac is on his way up!" I yell over my shoulder as I round the corner of the door.

"Ah shit. Get out of here." He yells after me.

I ran back to the room I was supposed to be in and go to lock the door, but find it doesn't lock. So I grab a chair and wedge it under the door handle. I get my phone out and call Jay.

"Hey babe is everything okay?" He says, his voice coming through the speaker.

"I need you to come get me now." I say in a whisper.

"Why are you whispering?" He asks.

This time I say it a little louder, "I need you to come get me. Remember how I told you things didn't end well with my first LA boyfriend? He's here at the hospital."

"I'm on my way. " I can hear him running through the house

"Bring Jade for backup." I tell him then hang up.

We hang up and I back up sitting on the edge of the bed. I try to slow my breathing and calm myself down. A few moments later someone pumps the door handle trying to open the door. Then I hear a knock on the door. "Kai, I know you're in there. One of the nurses said I should thank the girl who helped calm my friend. When she gave your description, I knew it was you." I could hear his arrogance in his tone. I didn't move.

"Come on Kai! Open the door!" His knocks grew heavier and louder. "Come on baby you don't need to be afraid of me. I just want to talk." He says with a hidden undertone. A single tear goes down my cheek.

"Well if you're not gonna come out, I need to check on Louie. Goodbye for now love." He says, his voice trailing off.

I heard him walk away, his footsteps getting quieter and quieter. Hearing motorcycles outside, I get up and walk over to the window. I look out the window to see Jay and Jade pulling into the parking lot. I take a deep sigh of relief, walk over to the door, unlock and open the door. The doctor was standing there with his hand raised. He was about to knock when I opened the door.

"Ready for an x-ray?" He says, taking a step back so I would follow him to radiology. We walk over to radiology and I get the x-ray. Turns out Tango was right. They were badly bruised and three were fractured. Doctor Mason wanted to wrap my ribs for extra support, that hurt. Teo had to come in a car and switch vehicles with Jay since the doc said I shouldn't ride the motorcycle. And before we left, he gave me a prescription for some pain meds. Telling me to be careful because they were listed as a narcotic pain medicine.

Chapter 15

Flashback

We were in a bar, the type that also has a side for food. There was barely anyone there, maybe five or six people other than us two. Isaac was drunk. He hadn't used all day. I could tell he was irritated so I kept my distance.

Isaac yells across the bar, "Kai gets over here." He slurred.

I slowly walk over. I get closer "Hurrrys your ass ups!" He lunges forward grabbing my shirt pulling me closer to him and almost falling. "Bartender we needs us some shots."

"Nice try buddy she's underage. And you are cutoff."

"The fuck you think you are?!" Isaac gets angry and I back up out of his swinging distance. He turns around and gets off his stool stumbling, "This is your fault! If you would've stayed at the fuckin apartment this wouldn't have happened!"

I backup farther from him closer to the back wall.

"I didn't do anything." I say almost in a whisper.

"YOUR FAULT!" He shouts as he grabs his beer glass and chucks it at me.

I duck going into a crouching position covering my head with my arms. The glass shattered against the wall and glass shards went everywhere.

Isaac stumbles out of the bar and I hear someone say, "Don't move miss you are covered in glass."

I feel someone start picking the pieces of glass out. I lift my head and lower my arms. I had small cuts and scratches all over my arm and a few on my face. They are small, they will heal and not leave any scars. A guy who was at the restaurant part of the bar gave me a ride back to his sister's place, saying it wasn't safe to go back to the same apartment as Isaac.

The next morning, I tried to stall as long as I could. Eventually I went back to the apartment and took a shower. I get out of the shower and wrap a towel around myself. I go walk into the master bedroom and start to get dressed. I put on a bra, underwear, short shorts and a tank top, then grab a sweatshirt to put on later to cover my arms. I hear someone walk into the room behind me. "Where the fuck have you been?"

"I stayed at a friend's house." I say as I slide past Isaac.

I grab my phone and keys and start to head toward the door. "Where do you think you are going?" He grabs my arm spinning me around. I look behind him and there is Coke on the table. *You gotta be kidding me,* I think to myself, *he's gonna be amped.* I try to say as gently as possible; "I have a meeting at the club I need to go to and I can't be late."

"I don't give a fuck, we are talking." He spews out.

I push him off of me and walk towards the door. I go to grab the handle and am slammed against it from behind, I slump to the ground. Isaac starts yelling, not making any sense. He pulls me up and slams me against the wall holding me against it with his hand around my throat. It's at this moment that I decide to fight back. Just like they teach you in defense class, I grab his wrist with my right hand pushing it down. Then using body momentum, I bring my left arm up in the air and bring it down on his forearm. His hand loses its grip and still holding his wrist with my right hand, then twist his arm around behind his back. I yell at him, "ISAAC STOP!"

He screams and pushes backwards, slamming me into the wall. Knocking the picture frame on the wall down, sending it crashing to the floor.

He turns around and punches me once in the face, then in the stomach, then in the face again. I drop to my hands and knees. He goes to kick me in the side but I catch his leg under my arm in my armpit with my left arm and punch him in the nuts. He stumbles back with a groan. He then turns his aggression toward the apartment.

Flipping tables, bookcases, breaking dishes and knocking the tv off its stand. He stops in the kitchen and screams, then yells; "I can't believe you! Look at what you made me do! Look what you've done!" And with that he storms out of the apartment. I cry and lay on the floor awhile not moving. About twenty minutes later, I get up and get another shower washing the new cuts and bloody nose. I get out of the shower and put on a bra, underwear, t shirt and jeans and a hoodie to cover my arms. I go back to the bathroom and try to cover up the bruises as much as I can like I have done several times before. I throw away my white tank top and walk out the door.

I call a cab and ride to the club. I missed the meeting and only a few of the guys were still there.

"Kai you're late. Hey haven't seen you wear that much makeup in a while." Alex says. He looks at me for a moment then shakes his head "You can go. Come back tomorrow when the boss is back."

Later that night I was in pajamas watching a movie. I didn't even bother to clean up the mess from earlier. I hear a knock on my door. I look through the peephole and Justin and Alex from the club. Crap I don't have makeup on. "We know you are in there Kai. Open the door."

"It's not a good time guys." I say weakly.

"You can either open the door or I can kick it in." Justin says.

I open the door and let them in, closing it behind them. Justin looks at me and grabs my chin turning my face left then right so he can look at the bruises and my split lip.

"Did Isaac do this?" I don't even bother to lie; he would see right through it. I nod my head. He lets go of my chin and walks over sitting on the couch. Alex sits down as well. I sit in between them.

"Is this the first time?" Alex gets out in a whisper.

"No." I say weakly.

"I should shoot him." Justin says angrily.

"No! You would go to jail. Look he was high and mad about last night." I tell them.

Alex interrupted me, "What happened last night"

I explain to them what happened the night before then go back to what I was saying. "I appreciate the thought, but you can't shoot him. I'll be fine, I'll figure this out."

Alex got more and more upset. "Let me guess the vase of roses and chocolates on the counter are from him? He says he loves you and apologizes. Promises it won't happen again. And begs you to forgive him. And it doesn't happen for a while until it does!" I stare and the four droplets of blood on the white shag rug but don't say anything for a while.

"He'd be so angry if I tried to leave. I don't know what he would do." I say quietly.

"We are not going to find out. We will go pack your things and you write him a letter explaining why you left. I'm sure he will figure it out. And leave it on the counter when we leave. Jade has a spare bedroom and you will stay there for a while." Alex responds. I nod my head and grab a pen and paper. I put the coffee table back where it goes and left the letter on the coffee table. And then we left.

End of flashback.

Chapter 16

Present.

Jay pulls up into the driveway. It's still raining, more like pouring. I go to grab the door handle but Jay tells me to wait. He grabs an umbrella and opens it as he gets out. He runs around the car and opens the door helping me out. We walk up the driveway and unlock the door. We walk in and I go to walk in the kitchen. I see a bunch of towels and other stuff covered in Melody's blood. I stand there looking at it and picking at my hospital bracelet but don't take it off.

"Have you heard anything about Melody?" I ask.

Jay walks up behind me, "Last I heard, she's still in surgery. Babe why don't you go upstairs, get into comfy clothes and watch some Netflix. I'll make us some lunch then come join you." I nod and walk upstairs.

We stayed in bed all day watching Netflix. Eventually Jay sighs muting the tv.

"Babe! They are about to reveal who the robbers are!" I exclaim. He smiles then pauses it. I look at him.

"Tell me about this dangerous ex?" He whispers out.

I sigh leaning into his side and he puts an arm around my shoulders.

"Tell me, I can handle it." He says gently.

So I tell him. I tell him about how Isaac was the sweetest the first few months. Then how he started using again and would have bad mood swings. How he would leave me with bruises and cuts then apologize the next day when he was sober, saying he loved me and it would never happen again, but it did happen again. I told him about the time he broke my leg and I had to lie to a doctor saying I was clumsy and fell down some stairs. Jay was silent for a while. I tried to break the tense feels; "And don't worry

you are much better in bed than he could ever hope to be."
He smiled but it didn't reach the rest of his face.

"Babe it's in the past. Nothing we can do about it now." I say as I rub his arm.

"I know but it makes me so angry thinking about someone hurting you like that. Men are supposed to love and protect their women, not abuse them."

I hug him, putting my head on his chest. He wraps his arms around me and we stay like that for a while.

Three hours later

We were still in bed watching tv and we hear honking horns and tire screeching. I slowly hop out of our bed and walk over to the window. Moving the curtain aside, I look out.

"There's a dog in the road. We have to go out and help." I tell him.

I don't even wait for him to respond, I walk out of the room and down the stairs. Walking out the door, I grab a hoodie off the coat rack next to the door. The car didn't stop, but he was in the grass near our mailbox at the end of the driveway. I get half way down the driveway and stop, bending down into a crouching position. I got a little bit of pain from my ribs, but it wasn't too bad since those pills the doctor gave me. It was getting late, the sun was starting to set.

"Hey cutie, what are you doin?" I say in a high voice and make some kissy sounds.

He looks over at me wagging his tail. I call him over and pat my leg and he comes running over to me and sits in front of me giving me kisses and squirming around. He was so happy to see a friendly person. I could tell he was an Alaskan Malamute. He was soaked through and muddy due to the rain. Walking towards the front door, I pat my hip so he will follow me in and he is right on my heels. We wrap a towel around him and Jay picks him up and carries him upstairs to our bathroom. We put him in the tub and give him a bath. We washed him a couple times until the water coming off of him was no longer brown. We turned off the water and he shook, getting water everywhere. I laughed and wrapped a towel around him. Rubbing him with the towel to dry him off, he licked my nose and I smiled. Jay saw where this was going.

"Don't even think about it. We can't keep him." He tells me.

"But look how sweet he is." I protest.

"He has a collar on. He belongs to someone." He reasons.

"You know how long I've wanted to get a dog! His owners can't be that responsible if he was out on the street like he was. That car could have hit him." I argue.

"Dogs get out all the time, it's usually an accident. Baby I know how badly you want a dog, but we just don't have time for one right now." He says gently. Then continues, "I'm gonna call the number on his tag and then we will go from there." He says then stands up.

"You know when we get married, you better get me a dog." I say as he walks away and he stops and turns around.

"Of course I will babe." He says with a wink, then walks out phone in hand.

About fifteen minutes later, Jay comes back into the bedroom. At this point, the dog and I were up on the bed eating some snacks together. Jay walks over and laughs with a sigh, then sits on the edge of the bed. The dog, whose tag says his name is Eli, army crawls towards Jay asking for some pets. Jay scratches between his ears and Eli wags his tail.

"I got a hold of his owner. Her name is Marie. She is so happy to hear he is safe with us, she has been so worried about him." He starts.

"How did he get out?" I ask.

"Four days ago, their house was broken into while she was at work. They stole a bunch of their stuff, including Eli. Which is probably how he got two hours away from his house." He says.

"Well now I would feel bad keeping him, she seems to really care about him." I say sadly, patting the bed so he will come over to me. He army crawls over to me again and rolls over on his side, resting his head in my lap.

"I gave her our address, she says she will be here as soon as she can. Her nav system on her car says the drive will take about two and a half hours. So she will be here at about two am. Maybe you shouldn't let the dog sleep in the bed with us? You'll get too attached." He says.

"Too late." I say with a sad smile, while stroking Eli's back.

Later that night, Jays phone dings and he shakes my shoulder waking me up. He gets out of bed and puts on pajama pants and a white t-shirt.

He walks around to my side of the bed and sighs, "So much for not letting him sleep in the bed. Marie is out front"

I had let Eli in the bed, he was laying with his back against my stomach and legs, under the covers. I kiss his head and pull the covers away. Putting on some shorts, I follow them down the stairs. Jay unlocks the front door and a woman about thirty, is standing on the other side.

She squeals and dives down wrapping Eli in a hug. He is clearly very happy to see her, his tail is wagging, he's winning and he can't sit still. She puts him on a leash, then stands up. She jumps forward pulling me into a big hug. I lightly pat her back a few times and she lets go, then hugs Jay and then leaves.

I sit down on the front steps and watch them leave. Their tail lights glow slowly disappearing off into the dark. Jay nudges my shoulder after a few minutes.

"Babe please don't be sad. He wasn't ours to keep. Let's go back upstairs and go to bed." He says.

I don't say anything but get up and walk into the house. As I walk up the stairs, I hear Jay close and lock the front door. His footsteps are heavy on the carpeted stairs. Once in the bedroom, I kick off my shorts and crawl into bed, as does Jay.

Chapter 17

The next day, I wake up and Jay is still sleeping next to me. I had forgotten he was off today. I gently grab his wrist and slide his arm off my shoulder. Sitting up, I painfully stretch my arms out over my head and my shoulder cracks. I look over to the clock on the nightstand, it was six thirty in the morning. I very slowly scoot over and climb out of bed. I get dressed putting on underwear, black jeans, a black with silver studded belt, a bra, a long sleeve white undershirt with a black t-shirt over it. I go into the bathroom and as I continue to get ready my phone buzzes. I walk out of the bathroom and pick up my phone and read it. It was from Ty; "u up?"

"Ya getting ready for the day." I respond.

"Good I'm out front in my Camaro". He types.

"Be ready in five". I text back.

"K." He responds.

I finish getting ready and put on my Wolves vest then walk out of the room closing the door behind me quietly. I walk down the stairs and out the door.

He is parked on the street and is leaning up against the side of his car. I walk up and he gives me a smirk.

"What are you smiling at?" I ask.

"I didn't know you were capable of getting up this early miss party girl." He says with a laugh.

"Oh shut up." I say as I punch his arm playfully. He chuckles again.

"The duffle bags are in the garage." I tell him. He doesn't say anything but follows me up the driveway.

Walking into the garage after the door opens, I point to the back of the garage where the padlocked storage lockers were. Ty had put them in there and locked it two weeks ago asking me to hold them there until the day before the delivery date, which was tomorrow. He unlocks it and takes four of the five bags, I carry the fifth.

Closing the garage, we walk back to the car and put the bags in the trunk. We both get in the car and he starts driving taking the scenic route to the club.

"I wonder when this rainy weather is going to let up." He says as he briefly glances up at the dark storm clouds through the windshield, then focusing back on the road.

"What, you don't like getting a little wet?" I say with a smirk.

He looks at me, raises his eyebrows and smiles but doesn't say anything looking back at the road. I turn the radio up and we don't say much the whole way to the club.

We pull up to the club parking lot at about eight a.m. and there's already a few cars and some motorcycles. I walk around the back and Ty calls out "Why are you going in through the back?"

"Because three of the five cars in the lot don't belong to anyone in the club. And I really don't feel like walking into any surprises in the front bar." I yell over my shoulder.

He nods and jogs to catch up to me and says, "Me either".

The club is a three story building, the main area was over a bar and restaurant. Bar and restaurant on the first floor, apartment on the second and club with an additional bar on the third floor.

We go through the side gate into the alley and go in through the back door that leads into the kitchen. The four dogs that are leashed up out back stand up and stretch wagging their tails once they recognize us. We go through the kitchen and I walk over to the pantry. I open the door and flip the light on. I reach up to the top shelf and pull out the log to check if the dogs have been fed yet or not. Seeing no checkmark on today's date, I put a checkmark and put it back. Pulling out the dog food and a jug of water, I walk back out back. I put two scoops of dog food in each bowl and fill their water bowls up. Seeing that they are happy and fed, I put everything back in the pantry then walk back into the kitchen. Ty is sitting on the counter eating a leftover burrito.

"People cook and make food on that counter you know." I tell him.

He shrugs his shoulders and keeps eating his burrito.

"Alright, I'm gonna go see if the boss is here." I say with a sigh. He nods but doesn't say anything. I walk up the stairs to the third floor. I push the double doors open and there are a bunch of guys I don't know standing around arguing with the boss of this branch, with Aj and Toby on either side. They all go quiet when the doors slam shut behind me.

"Kai this isn't a good time." The boss says with a sigh.

"I'm only five minutes early." I say looking around then continue "I have a package waiting for final checks before delivery."

"I totally forgot. Go back downstairs and have some breakfast. I will meet you down there as soon as I'm done here."

"Ya no problem Mr. Boss man" he smiles and I turn around to go back downstairs. I almost get to the door when someone steps in front of me. "Maybe she should stay, Alexander. She could be of some use."

Chapter 18

There was a clear and palpable tension in the air. Everyone was silent for a moment. Alexander stands up and breaks the silence, "Forget it Jeremy, she is not for sale."

"I never said she was. She is a person after all." He says not moving out of my way.

"Interesting comment for you to make given your primary line of business." Aj adds in under his breath.

Jeremy laughs and he pauses for a moment looking me over before he looks back at the boss. "Look Alexander, I only need to borrow a couple people for a couple of weeks, a month at the most. After the heist, we found out we had a snitch in our ranks who was talking to the twenty second street diamonds for a payout. I don't know if he is the only one, I need help from an outside source to sort out this rats nest. All I need is to borrow people to help me hunt him down so we can, well, talk."

"Ya I bet you're gonna do a whole lot more than talk." I say under my breath.

Jeremy didn't miss a beat, "Got somethin to say...Kai is it?"

"Not much, but why would we help a raven? Though you do seem more of a snake." I tease.

Aj cracks a hushed laugh but tries to hide it and gets slapped in the back of the head by Toby across the back of Alexander's chair. Alexander just sighs.

Jeremy takes a second but finally says "That doesn't seem to be any concern of yours. But if we could get back to the matters at hand, that would be great."

He tries to dismiss me but I get his attention. "It does seem to concern me given the little spat we had a few weeks ago. You know when some of your guys ended up leaving a blood stain on my friends' carpet." I tell him.

"They did that without permission. I have told them to move past it." He says with a sigh. He turns to Alexander, "If you help us out, we will give you a sizable chunk of that territory we have been battling for."

Chapter 19

Jeremy hands Alexander a file and he opens it flipping it open on his desk. He looks at it for a moment then looks over at me. "This is not a conversation for you to hear Kai. Why don't you sit on the couch over there and listen to some music?" I sit on the couch as they continue to argue. I put headphones on and turn the volume up. I watched them arguing and throwing their hands up in the air. This got boring after a while and I looked out the window.

After a few songs, I saw Alexander bang his fist on the table and noticed everyone had stopped talking. I took my headphones off. Alexander was pissed; "It's time for you to leave. I told you the most I will give you is four people for three weeks. If that is not good enough, you can leave."

Apparently that wasn't good enough for Jeremy. "After all the years we have known each other and the land at stake, you're gonna treat me like this?"

"Leave now!" Alexander says standing up.

"Perhaps he would like to be shown out by Karma. She's known to be quite persuasive." I say as I stand up

"Last chance Jeremy." Alexander warns.

"Am I supposed to be scared of you little wolf?" He says after he walks over and stands in front of me.

"Me? No but you will be when Karma bites you in the ass." I look over at Alexander and he nods. He picks up his desk phone. He dials the bar and tells the person on the other end "Let Karma loose." He waits, "Is it done? Good, thank you." He hangs up the phone and nods at me.

As soon as he does, I let out a loud whistle and Toby holds the door open. A few moments later our eighty pound Belgian Malinois dog comes running into the room.

119

"Karma come." I say and she jogs over to me and stands in between my legs. I point to Jeremy and say; "Karma watch him". She goes on alert and starts growling at him. I walk forward and she walks with me. Barking and showing off her teeth.

He raises his hands and starts to back up, "Ok, I'm going." Him and his three guys start to back up towards the door. As they are backing up Jeremy sighs, "I'll take the four people for three weeks. Call me later and we can coordinate". They back out and the door closes behind them. I reach down and pat Karma on the chest. "That's a good dog. Steak for you." I tell her, she wags her tail and licks my cheek.

I walk out of the club and down the stairs with Karma walking next to me. I go into the kitchen and grab a raw steak out of the fridge. I then walk into the side yard where the guard dog kennels were. We keep the trained guard dogs separate from the ones out back. I put the raw steak in her bowl and she starts to eat it. I walk out and close the door to her kennel. I go back in and upstairs knowing that I still have to get the delivery checked.

Chapter 20

I walk into the club on the third level and Alexander is sitting at his desk. He gets up and walks over to the table in the middle of the room. Ty had already brought the bags up. Alexander checks the bags, I stood out in the hall since I wasn't supposed to know what was in the bags. I was just back up in the car if Ty got in a tough spot during the delivery. I just knew that the bags were heavy and worth a lot of money.

Ty walks out with the bags and hands me one. We carry the bags out to the car and put them back in the trunk of the car.

"The delivery date was pushed to today. The buyer put in three grand extra to get it a day early. It's about a two and a half hour drive, we'll stop for burgers on the way back." Ty explains. I slide into the passenger seat as Ty puts a decoy cover over the bags. Once he's done, he gets in and starts the car.

About an hour later we are stopped at a red light and there is a pregnant woman waiting for the bus. She looks like she's about to pop. Three teenagers are sitting on the bench and not one of them offers their seat to her.

I started thinking about my first ultrasound when I was pregnant during my first week in London. It was three months into the pregnancy, I waited longer than I should have to get an ultrasound.

Flashback

I walked into the doctor's office and signed in. I waited maybe fifteen minutes until they called me in. The doctor was very nice, she said she would be there for me through the whole process and would even deliver the baby. She kept insisting that I call her Lisa instead of doc Tucker. "We are going to do a load of different tests first because you have waited so long to have your first ultrasound." She informed me. She had a nurse take some blood samples. "As she sends those in to run the tests, we can do the ultrasound. Lay back here and lift up your shirt please." She puts that blue gel on my stomach, it was warm, and grabs the remote wand, which she told me was called a 'transducer'. She starts the process and is doing her thing and I see her stop.

"Is something wrong?" I ask as I sit up on my elbows.

"No, nothing is wrong. Don't worry. Lay back." She takes some pictures, wipes off the gel, pulls my shirt down and helps me sit up. She was quiet for a moment thinking about something. That made me nervous.

"You say nothing is wrong but the look on your face tells me differently." I say.

"You are thinking about adoption correct?" She asks and I nod.

"I don't want to alarm you but there are four heartbeats." She says softly.

I was shocked but not at the same time. I sit there for a moment but finally say; "Multiple babies per pregnancy runs in my family. I am a triplet myself." I tell her.

"That makes sense. The adoption process becomes more complicated now. But to break it down they will be split into pairs like they are two sets of twins and will go to two different families." I nod and we continue the conversation.

End of Flashback.

Present.

The light turns green and Ty hits the gas. Still watching at least one of those boys was raised with manners. Getting up, he offers his seat to the pregnant woman who smiles, says something to him and sits down. They pass out of view as we continue to drive.

Chapter 21

The delivery went off without a hitch. We backed into a parking spot that was right behind the spot a van was backed into. I waited by my door and kept a lookout. Ty hopped out, looked around for a minute, then strolled to the back of the car. He opened the trunk and quickly moved the bags to the back of the open van doors. As soon as he was done, he closed the van doors and tapped the back twice with his fist. The van took off and we got back in our car. We were out of there in under three minutes.

On the way back from the delivery we stopped for burgers, fries and shakes. We finish ordering at the front counter and the bell for the door chimes. We turn to look and two cops walk in then sit down at a table. Ty casually pulls his zip up hoodie closed to better conceal the gun in the front of his waistband as he turns back towards the counter. We had left our vests in the car under a blanket so we wouldn't attract any unwanted attention.

"Will that be for here or to go?" She asks with a smile.

"To go." Ty says with a smile.

"Then your total for your order comes to $16.50." She says taking a twenty as Ty hands it to her. He walks away giving me a serious look then walks outside. The cashier hands me the change. I stick it in the tip jar and stand in the waiting area.

Finally getting the food, I walk outside and Ty puts out the cigarette he was smoking. We walk over to his car and I go to grab the keys. He pulls them out of my reach.

"Why does no one ever let me drive?" I ask, throwing up my left hand then letting it drop.

"Because you are a crazy driver. You only know how to drive fast. Plus your driver's license is suspended." He says as he gets into the driver's side.

We get in the car and pull out of the parking lot. "Want me to drop you off at the club or your house?"

"Well I don't have any business to attend to at the club, so if you could drop me off at my house?" I ask as I put our drinks in the cup holders.

We drive for about ten minutes, then pull into a beach parking lot so we can watch the waves while we eat.

Ty grabs his burger out of the bag and unwraps it. Tearing the bag in half, I use it as a holding container for the large order of fries that we are sharing and tear open two salt packets pouring them all over the fries. I take a drink from my Oreo shake, then put it back into the cup holder. I then grab my burger and take a few bites. After a few moments of silence, Ty says; "You were right, adding mayo to the burger makes it taste way better." I smile eating a couple fries then finishing off my burger, wiping mayo off the corner of my mouth and licking my fingers. Ty hands me a napkin.

Chapter 22

We pull up to the curb in front of the house. There were two big moving trucks in the driveway. I get out of the car, walk through the grass and walk through the front door. Dawson is in the kitchen making some chicken quesadillas. He pulls out more ingredients when he sees me.

"Dawson what's going on?" I ask.

"Expected news or surprise news first?" He replies, not looking up from the stove.

"Expected." I say.

"Melody is moving out." He says looking over at us.

"I kinda knew that was going to happen. What's the surprise news?"

"Colin is moving out." He says after a brief moment for suspense.

"Seriously?" I ask shocked.

"Yup. Turns out his dad is a governor of some southern state and when he found out where Colin was and what happened, he yanked him out of here." Dawson says still shocked.

"No way!" I say in disbelief.

"Yup. And get this, we already have someone applied and approved for Colin's room. He moves in tomorrow. Colin's stuff is already out so that just leaves the bed, tv and desk."

"Have you met the new guy yet?" I ask hopping up and sitting on the counter of the middle island.

"He looks like a blonde lumberjack, Kai. He is way different than anyone here. Older too. He's 34." Dawson says while flipping a quesadilla over.

"Well I guess now that Melody is moving out, we are going to need someone to fill in the 'responsible' role."

"We are all plenty responsible." He says. I raise an eyebrow with the 'you know what I mean' look.

"Ya I guess I know what you are saying. Your chicken queso is ready. And may I ask who your extra shadow is?" He nods to the doorway.

"Oh, this is Ty, he's a work friend. You can sit down by the way." Saying the last part over my shoulder.

"You have to work? It's game night." Dawson says looking sad.

"No, he just came to pick up some things I was gonna take to the goodwill. He's gonna try to sell them on ebay."

"Good, because your ass is gettin beat on the relay race tonight!" Dawson says as his face brightens.

"Oh ya right buddy. Before we start, we should outline new roommates' roles and duties before we party." I say.

He puts the quesadilla on a blue plate on the center counter next to a bowl of guacamole and sour cream.

"I'm gonna grab the goodwill stuff and walk him out." I say as I jump off the counter.

We walk into the garage and I open the garage door.

"Work friend?" Ty raises his eyebrows "Do they not know that you are in a gang?"

"Don't you mean a motorcycle club? And don't raise your eyebrows like that. You're gonna get wrinkles." I tease him.

"Seriously though. How much have you told them?" He asks.

"I like to keep my personal life and work life separate." I say simply with a shrug of the shoulders.

"So we're talking double life separate?" He clarifies.

"My boyfriend Jay knows."

"I don't know if that's the healthiest way to deal with work." He emphasizes the word work. I stop at the end of the driveway and he walks to his car and drives off. I walk back into the garage and into the house after closing the garage door.

Later that night.

Julian stands up on the patio table and announces, "This is the start of round five of game night and it is approximately 2:45 am!"

"Get down off that table before your drunk ass gets hurt fool!" Teo yells.

Julian ignores him, "Now I understand Kai and Dawson have been trash talkin each other all night about this round. Enough talkin! Let's get it on! Racers on your mark!"

We both walk over to the rope and Julian jumps off the table.

"Now this relay has four parts. Drink a beer shotgun style, run to the next checkpoint hula hoop for 45 seconds straight, run to the other end of the yard and drink another beer shotgun style, then run back. Got it? Oh and you have to dodge the solo cups full of beer or water being thrown at you." Julian says with a sly smile on his face.

We both nod and when he says go we both start running. By the time we are on the last leg of the race, we are both soaked in beer. I am winning when he grabs me around the waist and pulls me to the ground. He gets up and runs but I grab his ankle causing him to fall. We continue to go on like this with everyone cheering us on from the side lines. We inch forward, little by little, till we are just barely out of reach of the finish line. I mumble a sorry before I knee him in the groin and push myself halfway across the finish line. By this time, we are both covered in beer, grass and mud. I roll over onto my back and find myself looking up at a tall, blonde, handsome guy. Must be the new roommate.

Chapter 23

He stands there not looking very amused, with his arms across his chest. I stand up and take a few steps back.

"You must be the new roommate." I say with a little bit of slurred speech.

"I'm Colton, and you are?" he responds.

"Kai. And that guy groaning on the ground is Dawson." I say pointing at Dawson.

"I saw the responsibilities list y'all left me on the bed. Looks like I am the one who is going to be most responsible with utilities and bills." He says.

"You signed up for it when you signed the lease. I'm gonna go shower and get all this off of me. You can meet the others over by the pool and jacuzzi on the other side of the yard." I tell him, he nods and starts to walk away. I start to stumble towards the outdoor shower and as I do start to take my soaked clothes off. He stops and looks at me, "What are you doing? Aren't you going to wait until you get into the bathroom to do that?" He asks.

"No, that's a stupid question." I say with a snort laugh.

"Do you want to explain that logic?" He says, trying to hide a smirk.

"We have an outdoor shower. I am soaked in beer and mud. Why would I drag that into the house?" I say with a 'duh' tone.

He doesn't say anything but keeps watching me. I keep walking towards the shower and almost slip, once I get my balance I walk over and turn the water on. I take my shirt off and throw it to the side wadded up in a ball. I then take the cloth bandage off from around my ribs throwing it to the side as well. I then sit on the bench and struggle to pull my soaked jeans off.

"Are you gonna stand there watching me all day or go meet the others." I say still tugging at the right pant leg.

"Maybe later, I have stuff in my car I need to unload." He say. He turns around to give me some privacy and walks back into the house. I finally manage to get the soaked jeans off, but I leave my bra and underwear on. I get all the beer and mud off and use the shampoo that is there. I rinse everything off and then turn the water off. I wrap a towel around myself and go to walk into the house. As I'm walking towards the house, Colton is bringing a box outside.

"Stop. You are bleeding." Colton says putting the box down and grabbing my arm as I'm about to step into the house.

"What are you talking about?" I ask confused.

"You have a cut on the bottom of your foot." He bends forward picking me up bridal style and carries me into the kitchen placing me on the island counter with my foot over the sink. "I'll go grab my first aid kit." He says as he jogs off.

The cut must have been a decent size because there was a trail of blood droplets leading from outside to the counter. He comes back with a blanket, his first aid kit and a flashlight. He puts the blanket over my shoulders then moves to my foot.

"Looks like there is still a piece of glass in there, I'm gonna have to get it out." He says. He goes to clean it with some vodka and it stings so bad. I try to pull my foot away but he has a good grip of my ankle and holds it still.

"Aw man that stings." I complain.

"I have to clean it off before I try to dig the piece of glass out." He finishes cleaning it and then goes in with the tweezers. He pulls out a decent chunk of glass out, he holds it up in the air and a blood droplet drips off of it.

Riley had been sitting at the table, "Woah! How are you not throwing up or passing out! The man just dug glass out of you!"

Colton shakes his head and puts the glass chunk into a clear plastic cup. I pick up the cup and look at the piece of glass. It still has blood on it.

"How did I not feel that?" I ask twirling the chunk around the bottom of the clear plastic cup smearing the blood around the bottom of the cup.

"You were preoccupied and are pretty drunk. This is gonna need two or three stitches." He says as he looks at it.

"Who's gonna do that? You?" I ask.

"I grew up on a farm. That taught me how to do stitches on people and animals. I have a kit in my car. Wait here and put pressure on it until I get back."

Chapter 24

After Colton had stitched up and bandaged my foot, I folded the blanket putting it on the counter, then I went to go sit on the couch and watch tv. I fell asleep after about an hour or so.

I woke up the next morning and someone had put the blanket over me. I was still in my underwear and bra. *It's too early for people to be up!* I thought to myself. I flip over towards the couch and Jay walks over.

"Babe, you should get up and get something to eat." Jay says and I let out a grumble in response. He walks away and comes back with a bowl of cereal, coffee and a biscuit. He sets it down next to the couch and pulls my arms up to sit me up. He pulls the blanket off of me. He sighs and pulls off his white t-shirt and puts it over my head. He then pulls my arms through the arm holes. I lean against the side of the couch and curl up in a ball.

"Come on you gotta get up and move around. Stretch out your legs." I sit up and look down at the couch, it was laying on its back and I was sitting on the back part leaning against the seat part.

"What happened to the couch?" I ask.

"I don't know, you were on it like that when I got here. Here eat some cereal." Jay says as he tries to hand me the bowl.

"My stomach is in no mood to receive food right now." I say as I push it away.

He picks it up, crouches down and smiles "You have to eat something." He hands me the bowl then stands back up.

"I'm gonna go clean up the solo cups off the grass. I want that cereal to be eaten by the time I get back." He grabs a trash bag out of the pantry, walks through the kitchen and out the back door.

I look at the bowl of cereal in my hands. The bowl was black with a gold cat face on it. I pick up the spoon and watch the milk and cereal bits pour back into the bowl as I tip the spoon sideways. I feel something warm on my leg and knee. I look down and there is an adorable border collie leaning his head on my knee. I look around and notice no one is looking, so I put the bowl on the ground and let him have the cereal. I curl back into a ball on the couch and watch him eat it.

"I thought your boyfriend told you to eat it, not give it to my dog." Colton says walking in with a box of stuff.

The dog finishes the cereal and walks over to me. I pet him and he licks my nose.

"Do you know how long I have been trying to convince all the roommates we should get a house dog? I hope you are prepared to share him." I look at his tag "Ace. Did you like the cereal buddy? Huh?" I say to the dog and he wags his tail. I pat the couch and he jumps up and lays his front half over my legs.

"Well if you want to take him for walks, be my guest. His leash is on the coat rack but he is really good at recall, so he doesn't need it all the time." He says as he points to the hallway and walks away. I turn on the tv and turn it to the news.

About thirty minutes later the doorbell rings. Ace jumps off the couch and runs to the door. *Who is ringing the doorbell at seven in the morning?* I think to myself. I get up and limp towards the kitchen to check if anyone left a delivery note. Then limp to the door, my foot was pretty sore.

I look through the window and it's a pizza guy. I open the door, "Can I help you?"

"Someone called saying they wanted twelve large pizzas, all with different toppings delivered at exactly 7:18

in the morning. So here I am. The pizzas are in the car." He says.

I grab a large beach towel off of the bench next to the coat rack and wrap it around my waist. I walk onto the porch and down the front steps. Ace goes down the steps and off to the side to find a spot to do his business.

"Are you sure you have the right address? No one here ordered anything they would have put a note on the fridge like we usually..." I don't finish my sentence, I look across the street and Isaac is leaning up against the hood of his car.

"No, you tell him I don't want his fucking pizza and to stop stalking me!" I tell this poor confused pizza boy as I point towards the street. I walk back towards the house and call Ace to come into the house. I notice Colton by his car watching the whole exchange. I get back into the house and lock the door. I knew Colton had the garage door open and could still get in that way.

I walk over to the window in the front room and lean against the edge of the wall next to the window. I peak out moving the curtain slightly over. The pizza guy handed the pizza boxes to Colton and drove away. I look across the street and Isaac hadn't moved. He was looking right at me, he smiled, waved and got into his car finally driving away.

Colton walks in, "Why so hostile to our pizza donor? Who is that guy?"

"A monster." I say in a whisper, still watching the road.

"What's that?" He asks, he hadn't heard me.

"Nothing. He's no one." I say walking to the living room grabbing my coffee and biscuit and walking upstairs to my room.

Chapter 25

About a week later, I was having a late morning in bed and Jay walks in. He is all sweaty and is still in his work clothes.

"Another night shift babe? How many times is Talia going to ask you to cover for her this month?" I ask him.

"Cut her some slack, she is having a hard time. Plus I told her we can't keep covering for her, the boss is starting to get irritated." He replies.

"I'm not surprised." I say, eating another cube of watermelon.

"My brothers want us to come visit them in San Francisco this weekend because we haven't seen them in a couple of months." He says changing the subject.

"Now is not that great of a time. I got some stuff going on at the club, plus shifts at the club restaurant." I say.

"I know but when is it a good time? I'm sure one of the girls could cover your shifts for a few days." He argues.

"I guess we should book some flights." I say after a moment.

"Ya I will later. I'm going to take a shower." He says while he walks over to lock the bedroom door.

He starts to walk towards the bathroom, he stops in the doorway, "Want to join me?"

I smile and jump up walking into the bathroom with him.

25 minutes later.

Opening the bathroom window to let some of the heat and moisture out, I wipe away the fog and water droplets on the glass. The sky is overcast and there is a nice breeze. The breeze flows in blowing the curtains up a little as they slightly sway in the wind.

"Babe have seen my hairbrush?" I call out as I move to the sink.

"It should be in the drawer." He responds.

We got into pajamas since we didn't have any plans for the day. Today was one of my off days and Jay needed to catch up on some sleep. Jay falls asleep and I prop up some pillows on my side of the bed, so I can sit up in bed while doing some research. I go online on my laptop to book some tickets for this weekend to San Francisco.

He sleeps for about an hour and I look up ticket prices. I reach over to the night stand and grab a set of earbuds and my phone. I plug the earbuds into my cell phone and start listening to some music. I go back to checking all the different prices.

After finding a couple good prices, I remember that Teo had a friend that works on booking flights. He had said if we were ever going to fly anywhere to call him and he would hook us up. I pause the music on my phone, close my laptop and go to get out of bed to make the call in the other room so I wouldn't wake up Jay. I get halfway off the bed and a warm, bare arm reaches around my waist, pulling me back into bed and against his chest.

"Where you think you're going beautiful?" He says with a groggy voice.

"Sorry to wake you, you must be exhausted. I was going to make a call in the other room." I say quietly. He kisses my arm, nods and rolls over.

I get up and go downstairs to make the call. As I waited for him to answer, I looked out the back window and noticed that most of the roses had lost their petals. But one little fighter rose was still hanging in there. It was enjoying all the rain we had been getting.

I was glad I called Teo's friend, he got us two tickets in first class on a new plane. He said that it was usually for long overnight flights, but they were sending it to San Francisco for use. So while they had to send it over there anyway, they were allowing a limited number of passengers to book one time flights for the plane. He sent pictures of the plane he took a tour of and it was nice. He scored us a two person private cabin seat where there is a door that closes and the seats turn into a bed for long flights. It was only going to be a two hour flight but how often do you get someone offering you seats like this for 250 dollars a person.

We packed for a nine day trip, we decided we would spend five days in San Francisco and then fly to Las Vegas and spend four days there celebrating a friend of Mira's birthday. Mira called while we were packing and said that they were having a massive pool party at one of the hotels, all we had to do was book a room and a flight.

We were on the plane and it was really nice. We were both super excited because we had never been in first class on a plane before. We settle down in our seats and the plane continues to board and prepares to take off. The way our seats were arranged were facing each other, with a small table in between us, that would fold down if you wanted to pull out the bed. There was a sliding door on the side that you can close for privacy.

After we took off and leveled out, the seatbelt sign turned off. Jay was looking out the window and I locked the sliding door. He looks at me with a raised eyebrow and lowers the window shade. I lower the table and scoot forward pushing the button for the chairs to flatten out and turn into a bed. He smiles at me.

"Whatcha ya doin?" He asks.

"Have you ever heard of the mile high club babe?" I ask him.

"Loosely. Isn't that the thing where two people have sex on a plane?" He says with an even bigger smile.

"Well, we have this whole private cabin to ourselves. And what are the odds we are gonna have this opportunity again. This isn't something we would be able to do in coach." I say while I scoot forward and straddle his lap.

"Babe, you don't have to convince me to get laid." He says with a laugh.

I kiss his neck and pull his shirt off, then pull mine off. He stops me, "Wait isn't this considered a felony?"

"Only if we get caught. Lets just hope the stewardess doesn't knock for a while. And we have to do our best to try and be quiet." I say with a laugh. He smiles.

He kisses me deeply, while undoing my bra and unbuttoning my jeans.

20 minutes later.

We laid together, both out of breath. Jay pulled up the blanket I had pulled out of my carry on, up around me.

"So what do you want to talk about? We have about a little over a half hour left until we get to San Francisco." I ask.

"I don't know, how bout stuff so we get to know each other better." Jay replies

"Babe, we just had sex. I think we know each other pretty well." I tease him.

"You know what I mean silly." He says as he kisses me and pinches my butt, making me squeal laugh.

"Like what?" I ask with a laugh.

"How about scars? You ask me about one of mine and I ask you about one of yours. We go back and forth. I'll go first." He responds.

"Okay ask away." I tell him.

"How did you get that finger nail length scar on the side of your leg?" He asks.

"That's an easy one. I was thirteen, we got a puppy, she is a redbone coonhound. When she was about seven months old, I came home from a camping trip and she was super excited to see me. I had shorts on and she was jumping up at me and one of her nails caught the side of my leg." I explain.

"She sounds like a sweet dog." He says.

"Ya she is. She is eleven now, an older gal, she lives with my brother Jack." I say.

"Your turn to ask." He says.

"How did you get the pen length scar on the inside of your upper arm?" I ask.

"That's a funny story actually. I was out messing around with two of my brothers, it was past curfew. Well apparently we looked suspicious and a cop car turned on the lights trying to get us and we took off running. We jumped a fence and there was a sharp piece that snagged my arm. I thought it just ripped my shirt, I was wearing a dark flannel shirt, so I didn't see any blood but when we got home and I went to change, I saw the blood and washed it off to see how deep it was. My brother Lane patched it up and it healed leaving a small scar." He said with a smile.

"Sounds interesting. What's your next question?"

"What about this one…" He tucks my hair behind my ear. "This one, behind your ear that your hair partially covers and you can't see unless your hair is up in a high bun." He asks as he pushes my hair back and very lightly traces a line over the scar.

"That one's a little more depressing, you know my mom is a drinker, right? Well, when we were younger like nine, I guess we were making too much noise. She got irritated and threw an empty vodka bottle across the room and it shattered against the wall. Well most of it bounced off the wall into all different directions. The bottom piece flew at me hitting me in the head. It didn't knock me out, but I stumbled over and felt where the cut was. I was probably in shock seeing all the blood that was on my hand. My siblings, Johnny, Mira, Peter, Henry, Caiden, Luna, and Milos were all crying. They panicked when they all saw the blood. Jack and dad came in and quickly took control over the situation. Jack started picking up the pieces, while my dad held a cold damp cloth to the side of my head. That's actually the specific day my dad left her and we stayed in a hotel for a week." I said then was quiet for a moment. After a few moments of silence I shook my head and smiled. "Anyway, my turn to ask a question. Umm… what about that small one on the side of your ankle?" I ask.

"Ah that's the one I got the day we met. We were on that party boat and you were actually there with my half brother Romeo and his girlfriend remember? I was trying to impress you, doing a backflip off the high deck. Well even though I made it look effortless, I actually slipped a little and cut the side of my ankle on a sharp edge. Luckily there were no sharks and I got out of the water quickly. Romeo bandaged it up." He says with a smile.

"So that's why I couldn't find you for an hour. You were getting patched up." I say with a laugh.

"Your turn, what's your next question?" I ask him.

He paused for a moment. You could tell he was trying to figure out the right way to ask about the next one. I had a feeling that I knew which he was going to ask about next.

"You have told me that the scar on your shoulder was from when you got shot and it was part of the reason why you left New York. But you never really told me the story of it." He finally says.

I took a deep breath and was about to tell him. A knock was on the sliding door and someone tried to open it. I scream laugh and pull the blanket all the way up over my head so I'm completely covered. Jay chuckles.

"Right now's not a great time. Do you need something?" Jay calls out.

"Oh, so sorry to interrupt you two, but we are starting our descent. We are going to land and unboard soon. So we need our passengers to put all seats in the upright position and put your seatbelts on." The flight attendant says, then we can hear her walking away as her high heels click on the floor.

"I will tell you when we get to your brother's house and are settled in our room." I tell him.

He kisses me on the forehead and we sit up, grabbing our clothes, we get dressed and put the chairs back. Putting our seatbelts on after we sit down. I pull the shade up and we watch as the plane lands. We get our stuff together, then get off the plane once it is at the gate.

Chapter 26

Once we got to the airport, we took an rideshare to Jay's brother's house. Jay's brother Toby and his wife Riley were so happy to see us. We congratulated Riley on her pregnancy and once we visited a little, we went to hang out in our room for a while.

I patted the bed so Jay would sit down and I sat in the middle of the bed cross legged on the white sheets.

"The story about my scar on my shoulder is a little long. Are you sure you want to hear it?" He nods "Okay, please save all questions and comments until the end. If it gets too much for you just tell me and I'll stop." He puts his hand on my leg for a brief moment; "I'll be fine. I want to know."

So I start the story.

Flashback

I waited at the usual spot under the umbrellas next to the cafe. There was an outdoor area that was wrapped with lights around the poles that held up the metal roofing. This was where we would usually exchange money. Mira had come with me much to my protests. I told her she didn't need coffee at eight at night. She insisted, so I told her to wait inside.

I knew Nick had screwed up the previous meeting and even though I tried to fix it, somehow he turned it around on me, so I was in trouble. After about twenty minutes I saw a motorcycle pull up, I put the backpack down. But something wasn't right, he got off his bike but didn't take off his helmet. I knew then that I was in big trouble. I had decided earlier that this was going to be the last exchange with them. I thought that this is not how you treat those close to you and I was leaving the Red Daggers territory. Technically I was not an official member, so I was free to go if I wanted. But if I left, I would no longer be under their 'protection'. He stepped onto the curb but stopped there. He stared at me for a moment then reached for the back of his waistband. I reached for my gun in the back of my waistband and we both drew at the same time. I fired twice, hitting him In the leg and stomach. He fires once hitting me in the left shoulder. We both fell to the ground. He scrambled back to his motorcycle and took off as I crawled for cover. There was lots of screaming and people running. Mira ran over to me and started crying when she saw my shoulder.

"OH CRAP! WHAT DO I DO? HOW DO I HELP YOU?" She screamed with tears streaming down her face.

"We gotta get out of here, the cops will be here any minute." I tell her.

"WE HAVE TO GET YOU TO A HOSPITAL!" She says panicked.

"No hospital. Call dad, tell him we are going to a motel and we need help." She goes to pull out her phone, "Not yet. We gotta get out of here first".

She helped me up, practically dragged me up and helped me walk down the sidewalk. We pulled our hoodies up and continued walking.

"Mira how much cash do you have?" I ask her.

"About four hundred, I just took money out for party supplies for this weekend." She responds.

We get to the motel and get up to the front desk. We ask for a room and the guy looks at me. "We don't need any more trouble around here." He says looking down at a magazine.

I took two hundred dollars from Mira's hand and slid it across the desk, "This is for the no questions asked and no cops charge." The guy looks back up, looks around and takes the money, handing me a key for room twelve.

We walk out of the main office, across the parking lot and over to the room. She leans me against the wall as she fumbles with the key, trying to unlock it, her hands trembling. She finally gets the door open and she helps me inside. I walk to the bathroom and sit on the edge of the tub. I take a deep breath and pull off my forest green hoodie. I throw it in the too small trash can in the corner. I was wearing a white t-shirt underneath. It was soaked in blood all around the left shoulder and down the side. Looking around, I see a gray towel hanging on the rack. Pulling it down, I tie it as tight as I can around my shoulder while trying not to pass out. Once I've done this, I look up at Mira.

"Now what?" She asks.

"Call dad." I tell her.

End of Flashback

Present

"Are you okay so far?" I ask to check on Jay.

"Ya, I'm fine. Keep going." He reassures me.

I restart the story after taking a deep breath.

Flashback

Mira stands in the doorway as she looks through her phone. Naturally she is still really freaked out and panicked; hands still shaking. She finally finds his number and calls him. I hear what she is saying but she does not put it on speaker, so I only hear one side of the conversation.

"Dad! You have to get here now Kai's been shot in the shoulder." She pauses as he starts to talk.

"No, I don't know! We are at a motel. Please hurry, there is a lot of blood". She listens to his instructions. "Ya I will text you the address and room number". She hangs up.

"What did he say?" I ask.

"He said to stay calm, put pressure and don't answer the door for anyone but him." She replies.

About twenty minutes later there was a knock on the door. Mira looked at my gun on the sink but grabbed a fire extinguisher that was behind the toilet instead and went to go see who it was.

I was sitting in the bathtub with all the towels and the comforter from the bed. The comforter and towels were ruined and would need to be thrown out. The bathroom looked like a crime scene, a bloody handprint on the white sink, droplets of blood all over the bathroom floor, smeared blood on the shower curtains, blood on the edge of the tub, blood smear marks on the floor from blood soaked clothes and towels kicked to the corner. I sat in the tub on top of the comforter with it wrapped around my bottom half partially covering my lap and legs.

I use up a lot of saved energy getting out of the tub and standing up. I felt a little dizzy but grabbed my gun and stood in the doorway. Leaning against the doorframe, my arm was relaxed at my side, with my gun in hand. It was cold in the room but I had started to sweat. I struggled to stay standing up and felt like I was going to pass out.

Once I heard the door open, my father's voice and a 'she's in there' from Mira I relaxed. I put the gun on the tank of the toilet and sat back down in the tub.

My dad and a friend of his walk into the room. My dad walks over to me and kneels down unwrapping my shoulder.

"How you doin darlin'?" He looks at it while his friend makes a call.

"We gotta get this shirt off and assess the damage. This might hurt." He helps me lean forward and pulls my shirt off over my head, the tank top I had on underneath was soaked through with blood too. He grabs one of the towels and puts pressure on it. His friend walks back into the room.

"This is my friend Aaron, he is a doctor with a private practice. He's gonna fix you up. Don't you worry".

"I called for reinforcements including a clean up team for all this blood." Aaron says as he switches spots with my dad. He removes the towels, examines it, then wraps it back up.

"We need to get her out of the tub and on to a flat surface." Aarons says as he lays some plastic sheeting on the ground. They lift me out of the tub and lay me down, Aaron starts an IV and injects something into the wound, which stung pretty bad for a moment but then it stopped hurting. It turned out to be a through and through, so he cleaned out the wound, tied off some big bleeders, did some other stuff and stitched it up. When he was done, two women came into the room. They were close to my age, a little older in their late twenties. One was white and her arms were covered in tattoos and the other was Latina. The guys helped me up and then left the room. The woman with tattoos pulled the towels and comforter out of the tub putting it all on top of the plastic sheet. The Latina woman, whose name I learned was Mila, turned on the shower as I took off my jeans and underwear that were covered in blood on one side. Kicking them off onto the pile of towels and stepping into the shower. Mila helps me take off my bra and I step into the water. Looking down I watch all the bloody water go down the tub and into the drain. The two ladies help to clean all the blood off my skin. Once we are done with the shower, the tattooed girl wraps a towel around me, grabs the gun off the tank putting it into a bag after she unloads it and I sit on the counter. The doc comes back in and puts a bandage on my shoulder, then gives me two prescription bottles; antibiotics and painkillers.

Mila puts my wet hair into a bun and gives me a fresh set of clothes. She helps me get dressed and tells me I need to rest. I thanked both of them for all their help. I go to lay down in the bed and watch all the clean up people come and go with supplies and trash bags. By the time they are done, it's early morning and I had fallen asleep. I woke up when they closed the door. Mira was asleep next to me and my dad was doing something on his laptop. When the sun came up we all got up and got ready to go. I went into the bathroom and it looked like nothing had ever happened. Before we went out of the room my dad made me put a sling around my arm and we drove away in his car.

End of Flashback.

Present.

I look at Jay processing everything, I give him a few minutes to process. He doesn't say anything for a while. I put a hand on his knee to make sure he is ok and he finally looks at me with those brown eyes and says; "Thank you for telling me babe. I'm glad I know. Now I have another new reason to hate Nick." He smiles and sits up pulling me into a hug.

"We should get ready for dinner." I tell him. He smiles and rolls out of bed.

Chapter 27

I wore a dress with sleeves. The dress started out white on top, but faded into blue as it went down. Jay wore slacks, a nice buttoned black short sleeved shirt, tie and a suit jacket with the sleeves rolled up. It was going to be a large dinner with Jay's four brothers and three sisters coming, as well as his parents and any of his siblings' other halves. None of his cousins, aunts or uncles were coming.

The dinner was at his parents' house, so we rode in Toby and Riley's car. It was about a thirty minute ride and Jay and Toby talked about their jobs. Riley talked about how she hopes that the baby is not allergic to her dogs because she would be devastated if she had to rehome them. We pull up to Jay's parents long driveway and park behind Lane's Mercedes. We walk in and are greeted by all of his siblings and his parents. We say hi to Jay's mother and father, his dad insisting I call him Nate instead of

172

Nathan because he felt that was too formal. We sit down and Nate's staff serves us. The dinner consisted of salad as an appetizer, spaghetti and meatballs for dinner and a lava cake for dessert. The dinner conversation was light, Natalie, Jay's mother, clears her throat. Everyone stops talking and looks at her.

"I want to thank everyone for coming. I know some of you had to fly here to make this dinner. I do want to thank Tristen's wife Aubrey for making the arrangements for everyone to be here." Aubrey smiles and nods her head. Natalie continues, "I do apologize on your sister Amelia's behalf she was unable to attend because she is in Miami with her latest boyfriend."

Mason, Jay's youngest sibling gasps, "Mom! Are you calling Amelia a slut?"

Natalie pauses for a moment before answering, "No of course not honey! You know I love your sister. She just can be a little, oh what's the word I'm looking for?"

Nate gives her an answer. "Searching for a purpose."

"Your sister needs to find her purpose. And I would rather not hear the word slut coming from my seventeen year old's mouth by the way Mason". Natalie continues.

"You mean after all the partying. She is only twenty four you know." Mason replies.

"That's why we are giving her lots of time to figure out her path." His father continues

"Oh and don't forget our three half siblings that you didn't invite." Jay says without looking up from his plate. I reach over and pull his hand into my lap interlacing our fingers together.

His mother doesn't acknowledge his comment and continues with her speech.

"But the main reason we are all here is to talk about Jay taking a job at your father's firm. Toby you have already been to law school and I thought you could talk some sense into your brother."

Jay cuts her off "We have already talked about this. I am not going to law school and I am not going to work at a dad's firm."

"Why not?" Natalie cries out. "Your father makes such good money. Don't you want to make good money too?"

"I do just fine where I work." Jay says curtly as the staff serves everyone dessert.

It was chocolate lava cake with a scoop of vanilla ice cream on top, it tasted so good. I start to eat it quickly because I have a feeling that this conversation is derailing quickly.

"Working two jobs at a racetrack and a gas station? That's not acceptable! Are you just staying in LA for her? Do you even see this relationship lasting more than another year or two?" She motions towards me.

Jay stands up slowly and Natalie gulps. "I will not allow you to speak this way to either of us." He gets out in almost a whisper. "I plan to marry this girl. If you are not happy with that, then that's your problem and you don't have to come to the wedding. We are leaving." And with that he helps me out of my chair and we walk out. As we are walking out Toby hands Jay his keys "Lane can give us a ride home" Jay nods and says thanks then takes the keys.

We get in the car, he starts it and drives away. We were both quiet for a moment. Jay finally says something "I'm sorry you had to hear that."

I make a joke "I'm sorry we didn't get to finish our dessert. That was one good lava cake." We both start laughing. "But on a serious note, I didn't know your mom doesn't like me."

"It's not that she doesn't like you, she doesn't like that I broke up with the daughter of a wealthy family and messed up a business deal between our fathers. But we were not right for each other. Plus, I'm glad we broke up because if I hadn't broken up with her, I wouldn't have met you."

"So you want to marry me, huh?" I say with a smile after a moment.

"So is that a yes to my proposal?" He says with a big smile. He pulls over into a parking lot.

"Wanna do it in Vegas this week?" I smile even bigger

He smiles "Let's do it!" He leans over and kisses me and it turns into a make out session. After a minute or two we pull back and I tell him; "We should probably go before someone calls the cops."

As we drive, we both decide that we only want a few people there. When we get to Toby's house, we talk a little more about it. I got a notebook and started a list of who we want to invite. We decided to only invite a few people and then have a big reception later where we would invite our entire families. The people we invited to the Vegas wedding were Mira, my twin brothers Peter and Henry, Jay's brother Lane, his other brother Toby and his wife, and our roommates. We were happy when they each texted or called back that they could all make it. We packed our stuff back up and caught the next flight to Vegas.

Chapter 28

The wedding at a chapel was nice and quick. My twin brothers walked me down the aisle. Because Jay is half Latino the pastor said everything in English and then Spanish which added a personal touch. We were both so happy to be married. Before the wedding, the boys threw Jay a bachelor party and the girls threw me a bachelorette party. One of the first things we did was go to a jewelry store to pick out rings for each other. I picked out a beautiful silver band for Jay and gave it to Toby's wife since she would not be drinking. We all got pretty drunk, but were up by ten a.m. the next morning for the dress fitting. The wedding was at five p.m. and he looked so handsome standing there in his tux. He had got me a beautiful ring, it had a single diamond on a silver band. After the wedding we told everyone we would see them later.

We went back upstairs, once the elevator doors opened, Jay picked me up bridal style and carried me back to the room. Once we got there, we made love. After that we got ready to party.

We partied, went shopping and then partied some more. All of our roommates, my twin brothers, plus Toby and his wife went home after two days.

On Tuesday morning I woke up and looked over at Jay who was still asleep. We had been up all night, went to bed around four thirty or five in the morning. It was daylight out, the light cracked through the slits of the blinds. Jay was laying on his stomach, with his head turned to the side and his arms under the pillows. My phone buzzed and I slid out of bed. I picked up Jay's white t-shirt off the floor and put it on. I walk into the bathroom and sit on the toilet answering the phone.

"Hello?" I ask quietly.

"Hey newlywed. What are you up to?" Mira said through the phone. I could hear loud music in the background.

"I just woke up, Jay is still asleep." I whispered.

"Then put on a bathing suit and come join me at the pool. There is a huge party going on over here." She yells over the music.

"What time is it?" I say with a yawn.

"I don't know one or two. Get your but over here." She says hanging up.

I put on a black bikini, brushed my hair and put on some makeup. I Put a large t-shirt over it, slip on some flip flops and walk out the door with my phone, a keycard and sunglasses then quietly close the door behind me.

I get down to the pool and she wasn't wrong, there was a lot of people and loud music was playing over the speakers.

181

Mira sees me and runs over to me handing me a pina colada and saying "Take off your shirt and show off that new bikini I bought you." She looks at me for a second and then says "Don't be scared to show off your scar." And with that, she helps me take it off and throws it in the trash, pouring a discarded plate of nachos on top of it. "Now let's party!"

We went for a swim in the pool, then went up to the poolside bar where some guys bought us some drinks. A guy asks if I want to dance and I hold up my hand showing him my ring. He smiles and says "It's just a drink and a dance." My sister pulls my arm towards the shallow end of the pool where it has been claimed as a dance floor. We dance with the two guys from the bar and each other. After a couple of dances we are both a little drunk and Mira might be a little high, but we are having fun.

Chapter 29

An hour later a poolside waiter walks over to me "Is that your phone over there?" He asks.

"Why?" I ask.

"It's been blowing up. A whole bunch of missed calls." I thank him and he walks away.

I grab a clean towel off the back of the pool chair and dry off my hands then wrap it around my waist. I sit down looking at my phone. We had been down at the pool for four hours and in that four hours, I had five missed calls from Peter, three missed calls from Henry, two missed calls from Jade, a text from Jay, three texts from Peter, one text from Jade, two texts from Jack, and nine missed calls from my dad. Each left a voicemail each time which equaled nineteen voice mails and seven text messages.

Text from Jay:

1. "Hey babe, I saw your note on the coffee table. Thanks for leaving me some water and Advil on the nightstand. I will see you for dinner at 8:30 tonight, have fun with your sister today. And remember we are leaving first thing tomorrow morning"

Texts from Peter:

1. "Kai where are you? You were supposed to be back in LA like three days ago."

2. "Kai! You know we got shit planned! Henry and I can't cover for you for that long. We had that dinner with dad. He wants to know where you've been."

3. "I don't know if your phone is shut off or what but you have stuff you have to do here. You missed dad's big wedding rehearsal dinner. Dad's pissed."

Texts from Jade:

1. "I know you are having fun with your new hubby and sister but you have to get back here asap we got

lots going on. I had Jen cover your shifts at the restaurant."

Texts from Jack:

1. "You got fucking married! I don't even know what to do with you! How well do you even know this guy, you've been dating for less than two years?"
2. "Dad has been looking for you. I know you didn't forget about the agreement we made with him, family dinner when he is in town and that we would participate in his upcoming wedding. Dad is coming back from a business trip and is driving through Vegas for you and Mira. Be ready by today at four."

Well crap. I'd been so busy with being a newlywed on a honeymoon that I forgot about a lot of shit that was going on back in California. Well there's nothing I can do about it now, I will listen to all the voicemails later. It's five thirty now and I haven't heard anything from Jay about dad being up in the room. He must be delayed. I put my phone in Mira's bag, push the bag under the chair and join her back in the pool.

We swim up to the poolside bar and sit on the stools in the water. She orders us some shots. The bartender asks if we would like to try his specialty drink. Mira gets pulled off to dance with some guy and I offer to try his specialty drink. The drink was really good but he wouldn't tell me what was in it.

I turn around to watch people dance and off in the distance I see my dad and his assistant on the other side of the gate looking for us. I walk over to the fence and I don't even get one word out and he walks away. It's his assistant that says "Get your sister and meet us in the waiting area near the parking lot". My father doesn't say anything until we leave the pool area and are near the parking lot, "Stay here until I get back."

He goes to the valet and talks with one of the guys. They talk for a moment and then he hands the kid some cash and walks back towards us. His assistant walks over to a clothing stand and buys us two oversized shirts. The one he gives me is white with a black drawing of an eagle. The one he gives Mira is black with a gold drawing of a giraffe on it. We both put them on. Dad's assistant puts a hand on his shoulder "We've got a long drive ahead, let's get their stuff and get to the car". Dad looks down at my hand, grabs it, looks at the ring raising an eyebrow "We'll talk about this in the car".

We walk up to our rooms to pack up our stuff. Jay was shocked to see my dad, I walk over to Jay hugging him and he kisses my head while tucking me into his side. He looks up and holds out his hand in a greeting to my dad. He walks right by us, "Save it. Get yourself and your wife dressed and pack your shit. I will pack the stuff that is not in the bedroom." He looks around and the room was fairly messy. We pack our stuff, check out, get to the car and the five of us start to drive back to LA.

He rented a black SUV, so there was plenty of room in the car for all of us and our bags in the back. He sits me in the passenger seat, him in the driver's seat and Jay, Mira and his assistant in the backseat. We drove for a while until we finally pulled into a gas station. I had to pee so bad, I had my seat belt off as soon as I saw the driveway. As he pulled up to one of the lines at a pump, I open the door.

"For fuck sake Kai, at least let me stop the car first!" My dad yells.

"I have to pee!" I yell as I jump out of the car.

"I told you you shouldn't have drank all three of those slushies between Vegas and here!" He yells after me as he steps out of the car.

This earns a laugh from some college guys filling up their car. I don't reply, just run towards the store.

Chapter 30

Once I got back to the car, we drove the rest of the way back without stopping. My dad dropped Jay and I off at the house and then drove Mira home. I told him I had some stuff to do and he said that he would call in a couple of days. I walked into the house and put my stuff upstairs, Jay went into the bathroom to take a shower. I walked down the hall to Dawson's room. The door was already open so I knocked on the door as I walked in.

"Hey Kai, you're finally home. How was Vegas?" Dawson asks.

"It was good. Look, I know we definitely need to catch up and we will later this weekend at dinner; all the roommates will be there. But I need something from you now."

"Ya I understand you're a busy woman these days. What do you need?" He asks.

"Natasha's cell phone number." I say bluntly.

"Look if this is going to be some kind of retaliation or something…" he starts.

"It's not a retaliation, I just need to talk to her." I say cutting him off

"Fine. I'll text it to you."

"Thanks Dawson. I will see you later."

I walked out of his room, walked downstairs and called a cab. As I waited out front on the porch, I made a call. As soon as he picked up, I started talking "Hey I need a trace on a cell phone's location"

"What Kai, I don't get even a hi or how are you? I only hear from you when you need me to hack something?" He says sarcastically.

"You know it's not like that, Cassidy, but you are the club's go to tech guy. Would you rather me call someone else and pay them?"

"No, just give me the number." He says with a sigh. I read out the number and waited for him to do his thing.

"You know it still amazes me how many people don't turn off location services on their phones. I found the phone, I will text you the address." He says, I hear some taps.

"Thanks Cassidy, add it to the clubs tab." I hung up the phone and a few minutes later the rideshare car showed up. Cassidy texted me the address to a Cafe about twenty minutes away. The driver was fairly fast and we got there in fifteen minutes. I paid him then got out of the car grabbing my laptop bag. I walked into the cafe and looked around.

Natasha had this habit of always putting her hair in a high bun whenever she was out to eat food or drink coffee. She was in a booth facing away from the door. As I walked toward her booth the waitress was refilling her coffee. As soon as the waitress walked away, I quickly slid into the other end of the booth.

"Look Kai, I did not send those guys to your house after our fight." She stuttered as a look of panic crossed her face

"Why should I believe you?" I asked.

"I wouldn't do that! I always liked Melody, I would never have had my boyfriend or his crew hurt her." She paused looking down at her hands for a moment before looking back up at me. "Plus, I know it was stupid of me to try to fight you, I know I didn't have a chance of winning, but at least I got in a good tackle." She half smiled then looked down at her hands wrapped around her coffee mug.

The waitress came over, "Can I get you anything?"

"Coffee." I reply.

The waitress grabbed a mug and the coffee pot, filled my mug, then walked away. Natasha looked up at me for a moment, then looks down at her purse and riffles through it, eventually pulling out a purse size bottle of vodka.

"Want some?" She asks as she pours some in her own mug. I scoot my mug closer to her and she adds a little in. I pick up my mug and take a sip.

"You did get in a good tackle, cracked some ribs." I say after a moment and she started to apologize but I stopped her. "Dawson stood up for you, he said you didn't have anything to do with the break in. I trust Dawson, so let's move past this." She took a big sigh of relief. "I do need something from you though."

"What?" She asks hesitantly.

"Your boyfriend, he speaks Russian right?" I ask and she nods.

"Call him. Tell him to come over here. I have something I need him to translate."

She nods again and takes out her phone.

About twenty minutes later he walks through the door and slides in next to Natasha after taking off his leather jacket.

"Who's this?" He asks her.

"An old friend of mine. She needs you to translate something." Natasha says.

"What language?" He asks.

"From Russian to English. It's a recording." He nods and I pull out my laptop.

I play the video from our outside security camera. He watches it and reports "They talk going in and going out.

Going in they are just talking tactical stuff. Like how to go in, be quiet stuff like that."

"The second part. What did he say before I punched him?"

"He said 'say hello to your cousin for me'." I sighed and started to slide out of the booth.

"Do you know who he is talking about? For a friend of Natasha's, I could try to get you some information." He tells me.

"I appreciate that but I know who he is talking about. I only have one cousin who knows Russian. But you two would be good assets to have. If Natasha and I can be friends again that is." I look at Natasha as I stand up. She smiles "You never know when you could use an ally." She says as she shakes my hand. I go to set some money down for the coffee, but her boyfriend sticks his hand out and says "It's ok, the coffee is on us". I shake her boyfriend's hand and walk out of the cafe.

Chapter 31

I drove to my cousin's apartment the next morning. I knocked on the door and he opened it rather abruptly "If you need to borrow my sugar again..." He stopped talking when he saw me, a look of shock on his face.

"What are you doing here?" He asks.

"We need to talk." I say.

"This really isn't a good time." He says as he looks behind him then back at me.

I push past him "Is it ever a good time with you?" He had company. I smiled at them and walked into the kitchen. "Waffles anyone?" I ask. One of his guests stared at me with a look of surprise and interest, the other could care less.

"Y'all can finish up your conversation while I cook." I tell them.

I pulled out all the stuff to make waffles including his waffle iron. I made a whole stack enough for everyone to have some and for leftovers. As I walk over to the table, they get quiet. I sat down the syrup and waffles in the center of the table, then walked back over to the kitchen, grabbed a stack of cups and the pitcher of milk then carried them over to the table. I sat down, put butter and syrup on the waffles then started to eat them. My cousin stared at me for a moment with critical eyes then finally asked; "Not that I'm not happy to see you, but why are you here?"

"We need to talk. About business." I say after swallowing a mouthful of waffles.

"So you have said. Want to elaborate?" He asks.

I look at both of the other two sitting at both the ends of the table. Then across from me where my cousin was sitting. "Not until they leave."

"These are my business partners. You can talk about business in front of them."

"Fine. Why did Russians looking to send you a message, come to my house?" I paused for a moment then continued. "They stabbed one of my roommates, beat another. But they were looking for me, the others just got in their way." He looks at me a moment then sighs.

"I think you are over exaggerating." He says looking away, he looks uncomfortable. I turn my head to the side looking at him, then straighten out.

"What did you do?" I ask.

"Why do you think it's something I did." He says looking back at me.

"What did you do?" I repeated with a more serious tone.

"How about you stay out of my business and I'll stay out of yours." He says, clearly frustrated with the subject.

"What did you do?" I said for a third time, still serious but relaxed.

He slammed his fist on the table and yelled at me, his accent coming through.

"Careful cousin, your accent's showing." I said as I smiled.

"Cousin?" His business partner asked.

Both his business partners stood up "Look Ember, this sounds like this is family business. We can reschedule." Ember stands up and walks them to the door.

He closes the door behind them and leans his head on the door and groans, "You couldn't have picked a better time?"

"When would have been a good time?" I ask before taking another bite of waffle.

"If you would have called me first, I would have told you." He said in a tired tone.

"Why? So you can keep rescheduling?" I fired back.

"Seriously though. Why are you here?" He said in an annoyed tone.

"Because apparently, I have to clean up the mess you made!" I yelled the last part.

"Just stay out of it!" He yelled.

"I would have if I didn't have guys breaking into my house because of you." I tried to say calmly.

He briefly pinches the bridge of his nose and sighs, "It was a misunderstanding. I'll take care of it. They won't bother you again."

My phone started buzzing in my pocket. I pulled it out and walked out onto his balcony then answered;

"Hello?"

"Hey Kai!"

"Ty is that you?"

"Of course it's Ty! Where are you? We are leaving for the restaurant opening, I'm your ride remember? We have to be there early to help unload the food and alcohol boxes from the delivery truck"

"Oh man, I totally forgot about that. I'll text you the address to pick me up at." He doesn't say anything, he just hangs up the phone.

"I have to go cuz, please fix your problems before they come to my door again." I told him then finished the last few bites of waffle bent over the table. I walked by and he held the door open for me. Right before I walked past him he pulled me into a hug.

"I know I am rough on you sometimes, but it was good to see you despite the reason for the visit." I smiled at him as we pulled apart.

"Next time there is a problem like this, give me a heads up so I can be prepared". I tell him. He nods and I walk out of his apartment.

Chapter 32

I walked out the front door, then down the stairs and Ty's Camaro was parked out front. His passenger door opened and Ty stumbled out. I jumped forward to catch him before he fell.

"Ty? What's going on? Who's driving your car?" I helped him right himself before he tried to stand on his own.

"First of all nice to see you too. Second, for your information, it is irresponsible to drink and drive. And thirdly, I might be slightly intoxicated." He tells me while he struggles to stand up straight on his own.

"So who's driving your car?" As soon as I said that, a girl around twenty-five steps out of the driver door.

"Who are you?" I ask still confused but a little amused.

"I don't know but he gave me sixty bucks to drive his ass over here. Now he's your problem." She says handing me the keys and walking away.

"I guess I'm driving then." I say after watching her walk away for a moment.

"With a suspended license? Fine with me, at least we will get there fast." He says nonchalantly as he falls back into the passenger seat. And then he adds "You don't get to drive very often, so if you want to speed and drift go for it. Good thing it's been raining, the roads are still slick."

It had been a few months since I had been behind the wheel of a car. I walked around the back of the car slowly, sliding my hand across the side of the car as I walked. I slid into the driver's seat and sat there a moment, the smell of leather fills the air.

If I didn't want to attract attention to us I would go the speed limit and obey all the rules of the road. But how often is someone going to give me keys to an American muscle car and be okay with my type of driving.

"You're going to want to put your seatbelt on." I tell him as I put on my own.

Turning the key, the engine roars to life, ready for its power to be unleashed. I put my right hand on the gear shift near the cup holders and run my thumb over the rough stitching and it scratches against my skin. Putting my foot on the brake, I put it into gear and move my hands to the wheel. I feel the stitching under my fingers as I grip the wheel.

I can feel the car quivering in anticipation as I let off the gas. I pull out slowly, signaling, and slowly coast down the hill to the stop light, then slowly brake to a stop. He looks at me sideways, "You are kidding right?" I try to hide a smile but can't, we both laugh.

"Call Cassidy" I say with a laugh.

"He will freak out!" He says giggling.

"Plus that way we'll have a camera view on red lights and clear tunnels and stuff." I tell him.

"Ah smart." He says as he calls Cassidy putting it on speaker.

"Hello?" Cassidy answers.

"Cassidy, you hear that?" Ty asks and I start revving the engine

"Ya sounds like a car. What is that?" Cassidy asks.

"Cassidy! We are unleashing the racer!" Ty yells into the phone, which is met by more revving of the engine.

"What?! She has a suspended license for a reason." He yells through the phone.

"You got a few seconds to be our scout Cassidy, what's your decision?" I ask which is met by more engine revving and tire smoking.

"Smoke them suckers!" TY yells.

"Opening street cameras now." Cassidy says with a sigh.

There are no cars in front of us and we watch the light signal.

"Go on green!" Ty yells.

I stare at that light waiting for it to turn green. Our tires are smoking and as soon as the light turns green, we peel out. I take a hard right drifting around the corner. We make it onto a straight away and our speed just climbs and climbs.

"You got a red light coming up Kai. Either make this left or slow down and stop." Cassidy's voice comes through the phone.

Only to be met with Ty and I yelling "We don't know slow down!" And we both laugh.

"There's a gap you can make it!" Ty encourages, I push the gas pedal all the way to the floor and gun it towards the intersection. The gap was perfect, we blew through the intersection and made a hard left drifting through the intersection.

"When I said hard left I meant before the intersection! Not through the intersection!" Cassidy yells.

"Don't get your boxers in a twist Cassidy we made it just fine, there were barely even any cars." Ty teases.

"Cassidy maybe just leave the driving up to me. Ya know the professional street racer and person driving the car." I say sarcastically.

We continue to speed and weave in and out of traffic. We continue towards the bar and these two slow drivers refuse to pass each other. So I swerve into the emergency lane speed past and go around them while Ty flips them off.

"This is the last leg before we get there, you ready? Big curved tunnel coming up, perfect for drifting at high speeds." I tell Ty.

"Punch it!" He yells, hitting the roof of the car with his fist.

"Still there Cassidy?" I ask.

"Still on the line." He responds.

"It would be nice to know if the tunnel is clear." I say and we hear tapping on a keyboard.

"The tunnel is clear." He finally says.

As we enter the tunnel, Ty takes a deep breath bracing himself. We drift through the curve hard, the engine revving at peak capacity. We make it out of the tunnel and speed towards the restaurant.

"The bosses are gonna be pissed! Might as well finish big." Ty tells me. Instead of parking across the street, I see a spot right up front. I speed up, hit the brakes flipping a one eighty and sliding right into the spot, stopping against the curb.

"Like that?" I ask with a smirk.

"That was big." He smiles and hangs up his phone.

I turn off the car, we take off our seatbelts and step out of the car.

"You got a car cover in your trunk? Cops are gonna be looking for this car." I tell him.

He nods and we cover up the car. As we are covering up the car, I look up briefly and I can see Taj is in the restaurant on the other side of the glass door, with his arms crossed across his chest. He looks pissed.

Chapter 33

After getting an earful about driving with a suspended license, speeding and drifting, we were put to work helping unload the supply truck for the restaurant opening. Taj was so proud of his younger brother Vince for finally opening his own restaurant. Some members of the club who weren't busy decided to show support for Vince. Once everything was unloaded, we all grabbed a beer and settled down in the back room. A few hours later the place was packed. It was so loud in there that you had to yell to be heard. After some dinner, several beers, and several tequila shots, I walked outside to get some air. A guy from the club nicknamed Romeo was leaning against Ty's car smoking.

"I didn't see you in there." I nod over my shoulder. He looks at me a moment, blowing out a whole bunch of smoke slowly.

"I wasn't inside. I'm here for you." He says, taking another drag of his cigarette, the tattoos on his hand showing.

"You came all the way over here to tell me something?" I ask, a little wobbly on my feet. He blows out more smoke.

"No, came to pick you up. We have been recruited to find the snitch the Twenty Second Street Diamonds is paying." He says cooly, taking another drag of his cigarette. His neck tattoo showing underneath his leather jacket. He blows another breath of smoke out and stands up. He walks past me, throws his cigarette in an ashtray and walks toward his car.

"Let's go, you are not driving the Camaro again." Despite the nickname Romeo, he is not a guy you want to mess with. So it's best not to argue with him if you can avoid it. I get into the passenger seat of his car and he pulls out onto the street.

"I know we have had a long, difficult relationship between the Ravens and our group, but Alexander was clear. While this investigation is going on, we are at a ceasefire. We are trying to brew a new alliance with their gang. It's like a newborn baby, we have to nurture this new relationship. A lot of territory and money are at stake. So, I know you are not the biggest fan of them, but please do your best not to stir shit up." He says.

We are both quiet for a moment. I look over at him, he is staring straight ahead. One hand on the wheel and the other in the air, his elbow on the arm rest. He keeps twisting his wedding band around with his thumb bent under.

"How's Vanessa? She can't be too happy you are here and not with her." I ask him.

"She's fine. Her mom flew in from Chicago a few days ago, they needed some girl time." He replies, putting his other hand on the wheel.

"I couldn't help but feel a little bit of iciness between you two at dinner a few weeks ago." I say, trying to gently pull out some info.

"Look Kai, we are just going through a rough patch right now. We will get through it with time. Besides she's probably happy to have me out of her hair for a week." He says with a sigh.

"Is this still over that whole thing with Robyn kissing you? You stopped her immediately, V still doesn't trust you?" I ask.

He looks at me for a moment then back at the road, shaking his head he says "I should strangle Jen, I told her that in confidence."

"You know she only told me because she's worried about you." I tell him.

He doesn't reply and I get the feeling that he doesn't want to talk about it any further, so I don't say anything else, but roll the window down to get some fresh air.

We drive to a warehouse and the door is pulled up as we enter the driveway. We drive in and the door pulled down behind us. He turns the car off and we get out. I recognize one of the younger members of the club we are helping out.

"Well if it isn't the famous Sage Ryder." I say as I walk up to him.

"Hey Kai!" He says after he looks up at me and smiles. He stands up and hugs me. "I can't believe it! We used to hang out in high school!" He tells his friends.

"Kept him out of trouble all the time." I say sarcastically.

"Wait a minute, that is total BS." He says with a laugh.

"This little reunion is nice, but we have business to do." Romeo interrupts.

A guy walks up to the front of the room and introduces himself.

"My name is Joe, and I will be the main lead in this investigation. We have five members from the Wolves gang helping us out. We only have them for three weeks so we better work fast. Now I'm passing the mic to Romeo for updated information."

"We know that the person we are looking for is a younger male, anywhere from 18 to 25. He is supposedly really into sports. He is to be brought to Joe, here, unharmed. Is that understood?" No one answers but he continues, "Does anyone have any ideas on where we should start?" The room is quiet for a moment.

"If he is really into athletics and stuff, Kai and I are good at several sports including skateboarding, we could go around to some local spots. Try to get some intel." Sage speaks up breaking the silence.

"It's a start. Go over to the skate shop on the corner and get some gear. Keep me up to date." Romeo says after he thinks about it for a moment. And with that we leave the warehouse. We get two nice boards, each around eighty dollars. We also got pads for our hands.

We had been going from skate park to skate park gathering intel on this guy. It was hard only knowing the nickname the diamonds had given him. But we got plenty of intel. We decided we had earned a little skating around time and we were just cruising around. We took some steep turns putting those new hand pads to good use. We were going down this pretty steep hill and Sage was a ways ahead of me. There was a car stopped at a stop sign looking down at her phone. It looked like she was waiting for Sage to go first. But as soon as he entered the crosswalk, she hit her gas going through the intersection.

"Sage, look out!" I yelled but he saw it too late. She clipped the very back of his leg and board, sending him flying forward. She slammed on her breaks. I was going fast down this steep hill. I tried to slow down but only managed to turn the board sideways, falling back and sliding towards her car. I rotated sideways and slammed into the side of her low car. I laid there for a moment struggling to breathe. She opened her door and was freaking out.

"I'm so sorry! I only looked at my phone for a moment! I didn't see him!" I just groaned in response. She ran over to Sage who was barely moving. I slowly started to get up, my hoodie falling over my head and as soon as I'm standing up right, I push it off and walk over to them. She is starting to dial for an ambulance, so I grab her phone and throw it into the bushes.

"Why'd you do that? Now I have to go search for it." She says walking off.

"Oh shit you both took a hard hit." Another skater that had witnessed the whole thing came up to me.

I looked at him for a moment, then grabbed my skateboard; "Take this and get out of here. Sell it or keep it, it's up to you." He looks at me confused but doesn't say anything, he takes off board in hand and rides off.

It started to rain so I pulled my hoodie back up over my head. I dragged Sage up and put him on his board to roll him along. We walked away before she came back with her phone. The large apartment we were renting was close by so I walked us there. I had to drag him most of the way. We get to the apartment building and walk inside. The apartment we were renting had direct access to one of the stairwells.

"It has to be on the third floor doesn't it?" I say to Sage. I get him off the skateboard and kick it to the side. I start to drag him up the stairs "You have to help with this Sage!" I yell at him. We finally get to the apartment and I bang on the door. One of the guys opens the door and I walk in. I drag Sage over to one of the beds they had set up and dumped him on top of it. "He's a lot heavier than he looks." I say trying to catch my breath.

I back up against a nearby wall and slid down it. Sitting down I take some deep breaths.

"Call the doc, tell him we need him at this address. And tell him he needs a trauma kit." Joe called out to one of his guys.

I watch them rip his shirt off and assess the damage. They try to treat what they can before the doctor gets to the apartment.

"What happened?!" Romeo asks as he walks over to me but I don't answer him. I watch what they are doing for Sage. Romeo crouches down so he is at my eye level. He is about to ask me another question but he looks to the side of my hoodie and pushes the hood off.

"Call the doc back and tell him we have a second injured person" He calls out.

"Let's get her into the shower we need to rinse all this blood out of her hair to see where the cut is. It probably looks worse than it is. Scalp lacerations bleed a lot, even if they are small." One of the others says after he walks over.

They each grabbed one of my arms and drag me towards the shower. I stand up and swat their hands away, then I take off my hoodie.

"Looks like she has a little bit of road rash on the side of her forearm. We have to clean it, it still has pieces of gravel in it." The other guy reports as he slowly rolls my forearm back and forth examining it.

"She is wearing a white t-shirt are there any blood spots on it that would point to any other injuries?" Romeo asks, then they both look for a moment.

"On her forearm and hip." He looks at my arm and slightly lifts up my shirt.

"Looks like just a little road rash." The other guy confirms.

"Looks like her hoodie took most of the damages." Romeo says.

Turning on the water, we wait for it to get warm. Romeo tells me to sit on the toilet and lean over the tub. He pulls the handheld down and slowly washes the excess blood out of my hair and I watch as the red bloody water flows down the drain. They find a decent sized gash but not too deep. Turning the water off and wrapping my head in a towel, we wait for the doctor. The doctor comes in assessing the damage and stitches it up. He then gives them instructions on how to carefully get all the gravel out and to watch for signs of concussion, then goes to help Sage.

Chapter 34

The doctor had brought a portable monitor for Sage. He told the guys to watch him and make sure his vitals stayed steady. Turned out Sage had some pretty bad road rash, a broken right arm, and a collapsed lung that was reinflated, along with a couple broken ribs. After he was done helping Sage, he came over to look for any other injuries on me. He said he didn't think I had a concussion, but for the guys to keep an eye on me. He put a bandage on the road rash on my forearm and rechecked my stitches. In total I got twelve stitches to sew up the gash and two stitches in the top of my spit ear. He said my arm was badly bruised but not broken. He also said I would be sore for a few days.

After the doctor left, I went with some of the guys to get some food. We drove to an Italian restaurant about ten minutes away from the apartment. We got some Bianca bread and garlic knots for an appetizer. I got angel hair pasta with light sauce for the main course.

"Do you want to tell us what happened now?" Romeo asked.

"We were on our way back to the apartment. We figured we had earned some skating time." I looked over at Romeo and he told me to continue.

"We were going down this really steep hill really fast, Sage was way ahead of me. This woman was sitting at a stop sign looking at her phone. It looked like she was waiting for Sage to skate through the intersection. But as soon as he got halfway through the crosswalk, she hit her gas and sped through the intersection. She clipped him and he went flying forward, she then slammed on her brakes. I tried to slow down and turned my board sideways and fell back like you would with a snowboard. I slowed down a little but not enough and smacked sideways into her driver door. It took me a moment but I got up and got Sage back to the apartment."

"Do you think it was intentional? Maybe the Diamonds heard you two were asking around about their informant and sent a message." Joe asked.

"It's possible, but unlikely. She seemed really freaked out." I said, after eating the last bunch of spaghetti.

"She could have been a good actor." Romeo says lighting a cigarette.

My burner phone rang with an unknown number on the screen.

"Hello?" I answer.

"You the chick that was asking 'bout Vulture?" The voice asked.

"You got info on him?" I ask.

"Better than that, for five hundred bucks, I can give you his location." He says.

"I'll text you an address." I tell him.

"I would feel better if I picked the location. I will text it to you." He hangs up.

I let the guys know, we headed out after finishing our food and paying the bill. Two guys came with me and Romeo while the others went back to the warehouse.

We get to a motel and walk up to the room. We knock on the door, and after a few moments a guy answered the door and let us in.

"So you have some information for us?" I ask.

"Do you have my money?" He responds.

I pull out five hundred bucks that Joe had given us earlier and hold it out for him to take.

"Now that I think about it, this information is worth at least a thousand." He says with a smirk.

"We agreed on five hundred. Take the money and give us the info." I tell him.

He folds his arms and walks past me. I shake my head and walk over near the door and lean against the wall. Romeo walks over to him and punches him in the stomach.

"This can get really difficult for you really fast. Give me the info." The guy tries to swing at Romeo, but he misses. Big mistake. Romeo punches him in the face hard and he goes down.

"Grab his arms." He instructs the two guys that came with us. He takes his shirt off and puts it on a hanger in the closet. He grabs the ice bucket and walks over to me, "Go down the hall and get some ice".

I take the bucket and walk out of the room. I walk down the hallway and go to the ice machine at the end of the hall. I passed a window on the way and noticed it was still raining. I fill up the bucket of ice and walk back to the room. I knock on the door and Romeo opens it slightly. He takes the bucket of ice and hands me the car keys.

"Why don't you go wait out in the car while we finish up here." Without waiting for me to answer, he closes the door and I hear it lock.

I walked down the hall, then down the stairs to the lobby. It was pouring outside, I ran out to the car and got into the drivers side. I lock the door and turn the music on. It kept raining harder and harder. The windows had started to fog and after looking at the glass for a moment, I wrote 'broken' on the window with my index finger, wiping it with the side of my hand after a moment. After about forty five minutes there is a knock on the window. It's a cop shining his flashlight in. I roll the window down.

"Is there a problem officer?" I ask.

"It's raining so hard the parking lot is starting to flood. We are trying to move cars out of the main lot and onto the second-floor garage. Are you a guest here or just waiting for someone?"

"I'm waiting for a few friends. They shouldn't be very long." I tell him.

"Your fine to wait here but if they take longer than twenty minutes, please pull onto the second-floor parking area. Have a nice night." He says.

I see Romeo standing in the lobby waiting for the cop to leave.

"Have a nice night officer." I tell him and with that he leaves.

The guys wait a few moments, then run to the car. I unlock the doors and everyone but Romeo gets in. Romeo opens the driver door, "Nice try, you are not driving."

I get out and get in the back seat.

Chapter 35

We were driving back to the apartment and there was a lot of traffic. The apartment was about an hour and forty five minutes from the motel. It was bumper to bumper traffic.

"The road a few miles up is flooded. They are redirecting all traffic." I read off my phone, then continued to read the news update.

"There is a good hotel right over there we might as well pull over and get two rooms while they still have them." One of the guys says. The hotel was only two minutes away, so we went into the emergency lane and pulled into the parking lot. We parked on the third level of the parking garage. Then walked down the stairs to the lobby and up to the front desk.

"We would like two rooms please. Both with double queen beds." We told the lady behind the desk. She smiles and looks at her computer.

"I'm sorry but due to the flooding, we have only one room left. It is a double queen bed room, so there are two beds. Should I book you for the room?" The boys look at each other but don't say anything.

"We can share beds or someone can sleep on the floor. At least we will have pillows and blankets." I speak up.

The woman gives us a key card for room 438, we start to head to the elevator but Romeo hangs back asking the receptionist if they have any payphones outside. She points him in the general direction of one down the street.

"You guys go on up to the room, I'll be back in ten minutes." Romeo tells us.

Walking over to the elevator we step in and as the doors close I watch Romeo walk out into the rain, pulling his jacket up. Once we got up to the room, the guys turn on the TV and I go in the bathroom to get in the shower. Locking the door, I turn on the water and get in.

I got out of the shower, ringing out my hair and put it into a messy bun. I put on the same clothes but, always thinking ahead, I had a clean pair of underwear in my bag. Getting dressed, I could tell Romeo was back, I could hear his voice in the room.

Romeo and I decided to share a bed for the night. And the other two could decide what they were going to be doing.

"What are we going to sleep in?" One of the guys says.

"Whatever makes you comfortable." Romeo says.

I look at Romeo and smile. He takes off his shirt and hands it to me. I go into the bathroom, take off my shirt and bra folding them. Then I put on Romeo's big t-shirt and walk out of the bathroom.

Romeo is taking off his watch and putting it in his jean pockets. He takes the spot next to the nightstand on the bed and my spot is closest to the window and AC. I walk over to the other side by the window and lift up the comforter and sheet and get under the covers. Once I'm in bed, I slide my jeans off, fold them and put them on the floor next to the bed. Once Romeo and I both got settled I looked over at the other two guys. One was sitting on the edge of the bed and the other was sitting in the chair near the table in the corner.

"If you two are so weirded out, decide who is sleeping on the floor." I tell them. They both don't say anything. I sit up and look over at Romeo. He just rolls his eyes and shakes his head. I get up on my knees and reach over Romeo grabbing the room phone and call the front desk. Sitting down on the bed I wait for her to answer.

"Do you have any cots left? No? Then can I get five extra pillows, a sheet and a comforter? See you in a few minutes." I handed the phone to Romeo and he hung up the phone.

Five minutes later there is a knock on the door. The lady from the front desk comes in. She looks around, then says; "Let me guess you are going to make one of them a bed on the floor? I can make the bed for them. This will actually make it the 9th time tonight I have set up an extra bed." She makes the extra bed and leaves. We all lay down to get some rest.

After about two hours I still couldn't sleep. I slowly and carefully got out of the bed so I wouldn't wake Romeo up. I picked up my pants and walked into the bathroom. I used the restroom, put my pants on, put my hair back in a messy bun and then walked out of the bathroom. Grabbing my jacket and a key card, I walked out of the room slowly closing the door quietly behind me. I walked to the hotel lobby to see if their gift store was open. It was closed but the bar was open right off the lobby. There was no one at the bar except the bartender. I walked up and sat down.

"Can I get you something?" The bartender asks.

"Blended strawberry margarita and two shots of tequila."

The bartender sets down the drinks in front of me and walks towards the back room.

I threw back the first shot then took a sip of the margarita. I sat there sipping the margarita and watching it rain outside. I finished the margarita then threw back the second shot as the bartender came back. I asked for another margarita and two more shots of tequila. He made the drinks, sat them in front of me then walked back into the back. I did the same as the first set, threw back a shot then

234

started to drink the margarita. The second margarita was way stronger than the first but still good.

I was finishing my margarita when someone walked behind me putting their warm hand on my shoulder with their thumb up against the back of my neck. I turned my head to see who it was, it was Romeo. His hand slid off my shoulder as he leaned up sideways against the bar. He was just in jeans, he didn't have a shirt on, since I was wearing it, showing off all his tattoos and his six pack.

"What are you doing here?" He asks.

"Having a drink." I say taking the last gulp of margarita.

"I can see that. Why aren't you up stairs?" He asks.

"Couldn't sleep. So I decided to get a drink." I tell him.

"You didn't invite me?" He asks, pretending to be hurt. Briefly putting his hand over his chest.

"You were sleeping." I tell him.

"We should go back to the room and get some sleep. We have a lot to do tomorrow." He says after a moment then stands up.

"Let me finish my drink first." I say, but he grabs it and throws it back.

"Let's go." He says with a serious look.

I stand up and he puts some money on the counter for the drinks.

We walked back up to the floor our room was on. We slowly walked down the hallway silently. We got back to the room and I tried to open the door as slowly as possible so it wouldn't make too much noise. Romeo gets impatient and pushes the door open with a thud. The guys both shot up and looked our way. They both relaxed and laid back down when they saw it was just us. Romeo walks over to the bed, shrugs his jeans off, leaving them in a pile on the floor and gets into bed. I walk over to the other side of the bed, pull off my jeans, fold and toss them on the floor, then get into bed.

"Try to get some sleep and I will try to fall back asleep so we can wake up early tomorrow." He says then rolls over and turns off the lamp on the nightstand.

"Why did you come looking for me?" I say quietly. I scooted onto my side, laying my head on the pillow and looked over at him in the dark. He rolls back over and looks at me and sighs.

"I am supposed to look after you while we are on this trip. Plus I promised my brother, your husband, I would look after you. Now get some sleep so we can wake up early in the morning." He tells me.

"One more question. Why did you need to use a payphone?" I ask him.

"To call an ambulance for our uncooperative informant. I had already tossed my burner when I saw that cop. Now go to sleep." He rolls back over and falls asleep.

I flip over so my back is towards him and I'm facing the window. The curtains are drawn closed, they blow slightly back and forth in the current of the airflow from the AC unit. I was using three pillows, one under my head, hugging a second and a third in between my legs. I pull the sheet and comforter up to my neck, but poke my toes of my right foot out from the sheet to feel the AC on them. They quickly freeze and I pull them back under the covers.

Right before I'm about to fall asleep, a couple next door starts going at it. Romeo rolls over onto his back and groans. You can hear everything they are doing, thin walls. But must also be because we have adjoining doors between our rooms that has a gap at the bottom. Their bed is a squeaky one which just adds to all the noise. Every time she moans, he grunts soon after. This goes on for a few minutes. Getting closer to their finish line, they quicken their tempo. Their moans and grunts getting louder and the bed hits the wall. She starts moaning his name. They then both scream, finally hitting the finish line.

I put my hand over my mouth trying to stifle a laugh. Romeo doesn't bother, he busts out laughing and hits the wall screaming "That a boy Miles! Way to hit it!" The guys in the room with us start busting up laughing. The girl on the other side screams and yells "Pervert!"

"I'm sure the entire floor heard you Darlin'." Romeo yells back.

One of the guys gets up and quickly walks towards the bathroom, locks the door then turns the fan on.

"No, he's the perv." The other guy in the room jokes.

"Go back to sleep guys. We have an early morning tomorrow." Romeo says.

It's quiet for a moment but the guys start cracking up laughing again. I hit Romeo with a pillow and laugh. I roll back over then fall asleep.

Chapter 36

It was early in the morning and someone quickly opened the curtains on the window. I rolled over and groaned. Romeo slapped the side of my bare leg as he walked by and said, "Time to get up".

I sat up and sat there a moment. After a few minutes, I slid out of the bed, grabbed my clothes and walked into the bathroom. As I walked through the door, from behind me I hear Romeo say; "I got you a comb and toothbrush from the gift store. They are on the counter in a plastic bag so you can put them in your bag when you are done." I thank him for the brush and toothbrush, then walk into the bathroom. I get dressed and ready then walk out of the bathroom. As I walk over to grab my bag, I toss Romeo his shirt and he puts it on. Once everyone was ready, we headed out the door. The lobby was crowded with people trying to check out. Romeo grabs my bag off my shoulder.

"We will put the stuff in the car while you check out". Romeo says then walks off. After checking out I walked out to the car, it had stopped raining but it was still super cloudy and wet.

We stopped at a breakfast place that was on the way to the apartment. We were eating some pancakes and talking when my phone buzzed.

"I just got a text saying there is a guy in the alley with information about the Diamonds informant. I'll go out back and talk to him." I announce.

"I'll go with you..." One of the guys starts to get up.

"No, I got it. Finish your breakfast." He settles back in his seat and I get up walking towards the kitchen. I go out the back door and into the alley but there is no one there. I'm about to go back into the restaurant when I see a yellow folder on the ground, next to the dumpster. I walk over and pick up the folder and was about to open it when I am body slammed against the brick wall. I slid down the wall and landed on my side. I struggled to breath for a moment, I looked in front of me and there was a person standing there. At first I just saw his all black high-top Vans. After a moment I started to look up at the person in front of me, but before I looked up completely, he reached down, grabbed both sides of my jacket, and pulled me up; throwing me against the brick wall. He let go of one side of my jacket and put his hand over my mouth. I looked at his face and it was Isaac. I struggled against him and he smiled pushing his weight onto me.

"Now that's no way to greet your boyfriend is it?" He said with a sarcastic smile. I pushed him back and kneed him hard right in between the legs. He stumbled back but didn't fall. My gun is in the car, but the guys are closer. I started to run but he grabbed my arm with his right hand, spinning me around and back hand slapped me with his left. I fell to the ground and started to get up, but he hooked his foot under my leg and pulled it out from under me. I fell back onto my stomach and he flipped me over and knelt down, pinning me to the ground with a leg on both slides. I struggled to get out from under him and he put a hand around my throat, not squeezing but holding me there. I grabbed his wrist with my hands.

"This isn't how I wanted our first reunion to go." He says with a sigh.

"How did you find me here?" I asked him.

"The word is out on the street that a crew is looking for a snitch nicknamed Vulture. When I couldn't find you at your house, I figured you were part of the group. Plus with the flooding, I figured you would be in a hotel on this street." He uses his thumb to wipe off the blood from my split lip and wipes in on his jeans.

"You should go, the guys are expecting me to go in and finish breakfast pretty soon." I warn.

"Before we have the chance to catch up?" He stops talking and looks down at my hand.

"What is this?" He says picking my left hand off of his wrist. He looks at the ring on my finger but doesn't say anything for a moment.

"No, you can't marry him!" He says while removing his hand from around my neck and grabbing my wrist with one hand and pulling the ring off with the other. I take this opportunity to catch him off guard and buck him off of me. I jump up and run towards the street out of the alley. I get to the street and run right into a cop.

"Hey, slow down miss. Are you okay? Your lip is bleeding." The cop says.

"Officer, please help me. That man attacked me." I say pointing to Isaac. He takes off the moment he sees the cop.

"Stay here miss, we will get him." The cop says.

The cop and his partner both take off after him and I wait a moment before going into the restaurant. I quickly walk up to the table, "We have to go now!" I say in a low tone, out of breath. They all see the seriousness in my tone and split lip, they don't ask questions.

One of the guys puts a fifty dollar bill on the table and we leave.

We quickly walk towards the car, but slow down when we pass the cop car. We turn the corner and Romeo unlocks the car.

I stop right behind the car, bend over and puke right off the curb. Romeo hands me a water bottle and I rinse with it, spit it out, then get in the car. When we are in the car, I take a minute to try and catch my breath. No one talks the whole way back to the apartment. When we get back to the apartment, we all get out but Romeo doesn't. He rolls down the window. "Kai get in the passenger seat, we need to talk."

I wait for the guys to walk through the gate and up the stairs before I get in the car.

I'm quiet for a moment looking at my hand where my ring should be. He clears his throat and I look up at him.

"Want to tell me what happened?" He asks.

"Nothing happened. I'm fine." I say looking at the window.

"You and I both know that when a woman says she's fine, she is not fine." I don't say anything.

"You say nothing happened? Tell that to your split lip, messed up hair and missing ring. And not to mention you puked before getting into the car".

"Look, I'm just dealing with some personal stuff. We will talk about this later, I have a headache and I'm really not in the mood to talk about this right now". I don't wait for him to respond, I get out of the car and close the door. Walking away from the car, I run my hand through my messy hair and I let out a shaky breath.

By the time we had gotten back to the apartment it was past noon. We walk up to the apartment and put our stuff in a pile in the corner of the living room. I walk into the first bedroom to check on Sage. He seemed to be doing fine, so I let him get some rest. I walked back out to the living room and sat down on one of the bar stools. Romeo had made some scrambled eggs with toast and put them in front of me.

"Since you didn't get to finish breakfast." He says with a smile.

After I had brunch, I crashed on the couch. I was more exhausted than I realized. I woke up and it was after three p.m. So to wake up, I went to the indoor pool for a swim. It was a little cold but not too bad. There were only two other people in the pool and a couple teenagers in the hot tub. For a while, I laid on a pool raft but after about an hour I got out of the pool and rinsed off in the pool shower. I put on dry clothes in the locker room and as I walked out, ordered a rideshare. As I waited outside, there was a guy maybe twenty five smoking. He put his cigarette out and walked over towards me.

"Waiting for a rideshare?" He asks.

"Yep." I respond.

"My names Tony." He says sticking out his hand.

"Kai, nice to meet you, Tony." I say as I shake his hand.

"Where are you going?" He asks.

"A bar." I tell him.

"Well, I'm going to a party, if you want to share the rideshare, you can come to the party. It will be more fun than a bar." He offers.

"Sure, but to warn you I'm married." I warn.

"I have a girlfriend. So don't worry." He says with a smile.

About five minutes later the car shows up and we both get in. The address that Tony gave was about thirty minutes away.

We pulled up to a house and there were people and cars everywhere. Good thing we didn't drive; we wouldn't have been able to find parking.

Tony went off to find his girlfriend and I found my way to the kitchen, which had every counter packed full of different types of alcohol. Two drunk guys came into the kitchen.

"Hey I don't know you! That's not right! I must be a terrible host not knowing one of my guests." He hands me a shot glass, fills it with vodka and fills his with vodka and we both throw it back.

"Well I'm Travis, and if you need anything while you are here tonight, you just let me know." He says.

We each do two more shots then I grab a beer.

"There's so many people here, you probably won't know most of them." I tell him.

"Well that is true but I needed an excuse to buy you a drink!" He says throwing an arm around my shoulder.

"It seems the drinks are free here." I say taking a step forward to get his arm off but he also takes a step forward. Just as I am reaching up to push him away, Tony walks in and pulls Travis's arm off my shoulder, "Find another one man, she's married."

"I was just trying to be a good host." He says as he puts his hands up in defense.

"Then go be a good host over there." Tony says with a laugh as he pushes him out of the kitchen. I toss the empty beer bottle in the trash and grab another.

"So you are married huh?" I hear from behind me.

I turn around and Nick is standing in the entryway of the kitchen wearing jeans, converse shoes and a plain white t-shirt with a leather jacket over it. I can see the red dagger logo on the back of it in the reflection of a mirror behind him.

"So you didn't come all the way out here just to see me." I say sarcastically and he smiles but doesn't say anything.

"Not that it is any of your business, but Jay and I got married a couple of weeks ago while we were in Vegas." I tell him.

"What a special spot to pick." He says sarcastically then takes a swig of his beer.

"What are you doing here Nick? Are you stalking me now? Cause I think that position is already taken by another of my exes." I say then take a long swig from my beer.

"I didn't even know you were even going to be here." He says defensively.

"So then, what are you doing here?" I ask.

"Meeting with a contact, Tony. We are trying to set up a distribution chain."

"You're a little far from New York. This isn't your territory."

"I know that. We aren't doing it here. We are trying to get a meeting with Tony's brother."

"We?" I ask.

"Marcus and Jake are here too. Along with a prospect. Don't worry they won't tell anyone they saw you here. Please don't interfere with our meeting."

"Good to know. You want this to go smoothly? Then do me a favor, keep Marcus away from me." I say and he nods his head silently. I finish my drink and grab another beer then go out into the backyard. They had a bonfire going, people were roasting marshmallows and dancing to the same loud music playing inside the house, but it was slightly dulled outside. I went back inside and joined some people who were on the couches on the main level. We all talked for a while then Marcus came and sat next to me.

"Long time no see Kai!" I look over at him, take a swig of beer then get up from the couch and walk outside. He goes to follow me, but Nick quickly walks past and stops him.

People were roasting marshmallows around the fire while talking and drinking. Even though I didn't know any of them, they were easy to talk to.

We were talking about places we had visited. I started to get up and get another beer when another girl in the group offered to get me one since she was getting a few others one too.

"So you were born and raised in New York? How long have you been living in California?" One girl asked.

"For about three and a half years now." I answer.

"Wow. How have you been raised there, living here and not heard of Marcus Riley?" She says and they all giggle.

"Oh I know him. He's not all that everyone says he is. He can actually be a huge asshole when he doesn't get what he wants."

Kelly, the girl who offered to grab everyone beers, came back. "Here you go." She said as she handed each person their beer.

About an hour later I got up to go find a bathroom. I must have been more drunk than I thought because I had a hard time walking straight and felt really tired and weak.

I stumbled up the stairs and towards the hallway and went into the bathroom. I did my business, washed my hands and splashed some cold water on my face.

I walked out of the bathroom and started to walk down the hall. I was really tired so I leaned against the wall for some support to take a rest really quickly.

I started to walk down the hallway again with my hand on the wall because I was still having a hard time walking straight and the hallway seemed like it was swaying a little. I felt a strong pair of arms wrap around my abdomen and stomach. I didn't turn around but recognized his voice.

"You have to be more careful, you drank too much again. I can see you are still quite the partier or should I say alcoholic." He says.

"Marcus, get out of here." I tell him trying to push him off, he just holds on tighter.

"Aw don't be like that. I'm just trying to help you down the stairs so you don't fall."

I didn't have the energy to fight him. So he held onto me as we walked down the hallway. We were almost at the stairwell when he steers us into the second bedroom in the hallway. There was someone in front of the door, "Watch the door prospect."

"Nick won't like this." He protests.

"He'll be fine. If you don't tell him he won't find out." Marcus tells the other guy as we walk into the room.

"What if she tells him?" He asks unsure.

"Relax prospect, with the pills Kelly slipped into her drink she won't remember all of tonight when she wakes up in the morning. I've got to get going, the effect of those pills only lasts 45 minutes." He closes the door after this.

He lets go of me and my legs and arms feel so heavy at this point, I barely made it to the bed on my own. He takes off his jacket and walks over.

I started to fall asleep and I felt the bed move. I turned my head to the side and there was a person crawling onto the bed but he was blurry. I blinked a couple times and he came into focus, it was Marcus.

"Get out of here Marcus." I slurred.

"Oh come on, you don't want to have a little fun? You are the party girl, remember?"

"Out of here Marcus!" I say then push him away. He loses his balance and falls back.

I passed out briefly but woke up when I felt someone tugging at my jeans. He leaned over and kissed my cheek, then my shoulder through my shirt. He unbuttons the first three buttons of my plaid shirt and kisses my collarbone. I push his head back and roll into a ball on my side with my back towards him. I pass out again and when I wake up he is hovering over me. *Stay awake*, I think to myself *You have to fight*. He tried to kiss my lips but I moved my head sideways. I tried to push myself up but my arms felt so heavy, I couldn't lift them. "Get off of me, Marcus." I pushed the words out and it felt like trying to talk with a mouthful of pancakes drenched in syrup. He didn't reply, he just continued to slowly kiss me all over. I passed out again, when I came to, I was naked from the waste down and he was on top of me. I tried to focus on the words but nothing came out. I tried again and just managed "Gert off".

"That scar I gave you on your shoulder is real sexy". He says with an evil smile, pushes my shirt off my shoulder, then he licks it. I wanted to scream but no one would hear me over the loud music.

Looking for ways to get him off of me, I look over to the bedside table. There is a pair of large scissors with orange handles in a jar with some pens and highlighters. I look up at him and his eyes are closed, he's concentrating and moaning. My hand slowly moves over across the edge of the bed and onto the desk. I gather as much energy as I can and grab the scissors and in the same moment jammed them into his ribcage. He screams, falling off me and off the bed. The party music was loud outside, his prospect outside didn't hear it.

I was so tired, I couldn't move for a while. I rolled onto my side rolling up in a ball and passed out again. When I came to, the pills were starting to wear off already. It probably helped that I didn't finish that drink. I stumbled out of the bed, grabbed my clothes and with wobbly legs crawled into the bathroom. Trying not to panic, I tried to focus on slowing my breathing. I locked the bathroom door and sat on the bath mat for a while, before I felt like I could talk and move again somewhat normally. I pulled out my phone and looked through the contacts scrolling past several potentials, then saw Romeo's name. My thumb hovered over his name for a moment before clicking on his number hitting call. It seemed like he took so long to answer as each ringing tone seemed to take longer than the last. And by the time he answered I had already started to cry.

"Hello?" He answers.

"Hey, sorry I know it's late." I took a minute to gather my strong voice.

"It's ok, I'm still up working on some stuff for the manhunt. What do you need?"

I pause before answering and said "You know what never mind." my voice started to shake and he could hear it.

"Hey tell me what's going on." He says. I can hear his pen click and drop.

"You are on parole. I don't want to get you involved in a new mess. I'm fine, I'm just drunk at a party." I tell him.

"Do you need me to come get you?" He asks.

"Romeo something happened over here. I need help." I started to cry again.

"Send me the address. Me and some of the guys are on our way."

"Romeo, don't bring Jay, I don't want him to see this."

I got dressed while I waited, about twenty minutes later they came into the room and there were five of them. Three of them stopped in the bedroom, while Romeo and Jen came into the bathroom. Romeo and I had been friends for several months before I met Jay through Romeo. I knew I could count on Romeo when I needed help. Though they didn't talk about being half-brothers very often, they were always there for each other but given they had different moms, didn't look alike.

Jen comes in and sits on the edge of the tub next to me and tucks a stray strand of hair behind my ear, while Romeo stands in the doorway.

"What happened?" She asks after looking me over .

"He," I paused for a moment looking down. They were both patient and waited for me to continue. "I think he slipped something into my beer." I paused again, trying to gather my thoughts together, I was still fairly drunk. I started again, "I just ... I had to get out of there ... I had to get him off of me ... and the scissors were there. So I grabbed them and defended myself." I tell them. *They didn't need to know all the details,* I thought to myself. They are both quiet for a moment.

Jen turns to Romeo, "Romeo I'm gonna get her out of here."

"She needs to sleep here tonight." He says still in the doorway, leaning against the doorframe with his hands in his pockets.

"Are you crazy? We have to get her to a hospital." Jen says standing up.

Romeo stands up, "He is still alive right now. But if he doesn't stay that way, she can't be the last person to see him alive. They can't both leave at the same time."

"Get her cleaned up and the guys will get him to the club. We can't let the other club know anything is wrong, so we need to act normal. I'll get rid of his car. Wait for me to get back to the club before you do anything. Don't do anything you are gonna regret."

Romeo leaves and Jen pulls me off the toilet and into the tub. "Let's get cleaned up."

The next morning I wake up and look around the room and there are people passed out on the ground, on furniture, on the table, just all over the place. Getting up I feel sore all over, I walked towards the kitchen maneuvering around people, trying not to step on them.

Tony was in the kitchen drinking coffee. He smiled when he saw me "Have fun last night?"

I didn't answer, I just walked past him towards the fridge to get some water. I then walked over to an open couch and laid down. I felt someone shake my shoulder and I looked up. It was Jay's older brother.

"Lane?" I asked confused.

He kneeled down "How about we get you out of here." He helped me up and put my arm over his shoulder and his arm around my waist. And we walked to his car.

Chapter 37

Lane didn't say anything the whole way back from the party, other than to say he was my alibi for the morning. So I just looked out the window at the scenery and the passing cars. We stopped for breakfast and gas then went to see a movie. By the time he dropped me off at the apartment it was around one thirty. I walk up the stairs and open the door to the apartment. When I walk in, there is a lot of arguing going on. I close the door loudly and they stop arguing for a moment. Romeo gives me a fake pissed off look.

"Sit over there. I will deal with you later." Romeo was arguing with the doctor.

"We can't take him to a hospital and the pop up clinic is too far away." Romeo says.

"I can only do so much. There was a lot of damage done by that car hitting him. He has developed a serious infection. He needs special treatment and meds that I can't provide." The doctor says.

"I'm not going to discuss this with you anymore." Romeo takes a slow step towards him "Fix him." He says pointing towards Sage. His phone rings and he walks out onto the balcony. Sean, one of the guys from the other crew, gives me a look and we walk into the kitchen. Sean pours us both a cup of coffee. He hands it to me, "You know we need to do something to help Sage."

Romeo comes back into the room. "Joe just got a tip about where the Diamond's informant will be tonight at 11:40 tonight. We all have to go to the warehouse and talk strategies." Everyone starts to grab their stuff and I look towards the first bedroom and can see Sage's arm hanging off the side of the bed.

I look at Sean then speak up "I need to get a shower and make a few calls. Would it be ok if Sean waits for me and gives me a ride to the warehouse in about an hour?" I look over at Sean and he gets it.

"I don't mind waiting for her." He offers.

"Get in the shower now so you don't take so long." Romeo says.

I go and get undressed then hop in the shower turning on the water. I let the water run over my head and wait for them to leave. Sean comes in about five minutes later "They are gone, let's get him out of here."

I jump out of the shower and dry off. I was putting on a new pair of clothes when I heard a thud in the other room. I finish getting dressed and walk into the first bedroom. Sage had fallen out of the bed. I walked over to him, he had ripped his stitches and he had a fever.

"Help me get him up." Sean says.

He only had a pair of shorts on, so I grabbed a black zip up hoodie and ran out the door. Sean was trying to walk him down the stairs and decided it would be easier to carry him instead. "Get in the backseat, I'll lean him up against you." Sean says.

I climb into the backseat and he pours him in, then jumps into the driver's seat. He speeds out of the parking lot, weaves in and out of traffic and runs a few red lights. We pull up in front of the hospital and we pull him out. Sean said he would wait in the car so we could get out of there quickly. Hospitals means cops. I put Sage's arm over my shoulder and tried to walk him into the hospital. He could barely walk and I ended up practically dragging him. We walked in through the sliding doors and I look around. The emergency room was really crowded. I walked up to the front desk and tell the receptionist at the front desk "Excuse me miss, he needs help."

"Fill this out and take a seat." She says as she hands me a clipboard.

"He needs help now." I tell her trying to get her attention.

She doesn't pay any attention and starts typing on her computer then goes and refills her coffee cup.

I sit Sage down in a nearby chair and hop over the front desk counter. I walk down the hallway and open each door as I go down the hallway. Now I have the receptionists' attention.

"Miss you can't be back here! It's for employees and patients only." The receptionist urges.

I opened another door and there are a few people. "Are any of you a doctor?" I ask.

The receptionist came in behind me and grabbed my arm with one hand and the back of my shirt with the other.

"You can't be back here." She lets go of my shirt when she feels my gun in the back of my waistband.

I spin around and get right up in her face "Grabbing me like that might not be such a good idea for you." She let go of me and took a step back.

One of the doctors stepped forward "What seems to be the problem miss?"

"My friend was hit by a car and she doesn't seem to care." I say still staring at her.

"How long ago was this?" He has a new sense of urgency in his voice.

"A few days ago. We had a private doctor look at him but he is getting worse." I inform him.

"Take me to him now." The doctor says.

We walk out to the waiting room and three doctors and a whole bunch of nurses surround him and bring out a stretcher rolling him to the trauma bay. Once I know they are taking good care of him, I try to walk out of the hospital very quickly. I stop when I see someone familiar walk into the waiting room in cuffs escorted by a cop. He is sat down, cuffed to the chair, then the cop walks off. I walk over and sit across from him.

"You look comfortable." I say sarcastically.

"Trust me love, these handcuffs are not comfortable." He says.

"It is your fault you got arrested. You need help." I tell him. He doesn't say anything.

A cop comes over "They will see you in fifteen minutes. Miss, can I help you?"

"He has something that belongs to me." I tell him.

"And what is that exactly?" The cop asks.

"My wedding ring." I say.

"Ah I see". The cop pulls it out of his pocket and hands it to me. "So I take it you won't be pressing assault charges then."

I look at Isaac for a moment, then back at the cop "No, I won't be pressing charges".

"Well, he will be facing charges for assaulting an officer, running and resisting arrest. He will probably get six months to a year."

I stand up and look at him. I lean forward and grab his chin pulling his head up so he looks at me. "Take this seriously. You need to move on. I'm married now." I hold my hand up in the air and put my ring back on while he's watching, then turn around and walk away.

"See you in six months love." Isaac says. I stop for a moment but don't turn around. I start moving again and walk out of the hospital. I get back to the car and we drive to the warehouse.

Chapter 38

Once we got to the warehouse, everyone caught us up on the plan. The Diamonds' informant is supposed to be in a bar near the forest in Northern California, near the California – Oregon border. He was supposed to be receiving his last payment. Tino had driven up with Karma and Gunner two guard / attack dogs to help with the raid.

We drove up to the bar and pulled into the parking lot. We had all downloaded this app on our phones that turned our phones into two way radios so we could all communicate.

"Wait in the car. Report if you see him. Do not engage unless he shoots at you." Romeo tells me as they all start to get out. They all go in with their guns drawn and there is a lot of yelling and glass breaking. A bathroom window from the second floor opens and someone jumps out of it. He lands and rolls so he won't break an ankle or leg, then runs towards me.

"We have a runner! It has to be him!" I yell into the radio.

He runs past me and I immediately recognize him. I push the car door open and start to get out. As I'm getting out, another person jumps out of the window and roles similarly like the first, however I can tell this one is a woman. Seems that Vulture has an accomplice. She runs the opposite way, towards the back parking lot. As she is running she looks back to see if anyone is following her. In the neon light of the outside sign, I can see her face and recognize her as well.

"Do not engage! Wait for backup!" I hear Romeo urge as I'm getting out of the car. I throw my phone onto the seat and slam the door shut running after him. I can only follow one, so I chase him into the woods.

Chasing after him into the woods, I catch up and pull my gun.

"STOP!" I yell as I fire a shot into the ground making him stop. He turns around and looks at me. I can't bring myself to shoot him, so I just stand there with my gun drawn but at my side. Neither of us say anything for a while. We hear shouting and footsteps coming towards us.

"Do you have your kevlar vest on Kai?" He asks.

"Of course I do. We are on a raid, we wouldn't go on one without wearing them." I state.

As soon as I tell him I have it on, he shoots me twice in the vest, turns and runs. I fall backwards and hit the ground, the wind knocked out of me. It felt like getting hit in the ribs and chest with a spring loaded sledge hammer.

I stare up at the trees and see the trees and clouds with the stars peeking through. Towards the right, an owl stares down at me, his eyes so golden orange in the night light. It was like he was trying to tell me something; *'breathe! You need to breathe!'* I gasp for air and try to breathe. As I lay on the ground, flashlights come into view. My team sees me on the ground and start to look where I was hit. Romeo rips my buttoned outer shirt open and sees that both bullets hit me in the vest.

"Hey, you're ok. Just breathe. The bullets are stuck in your vest, they didn't go through." Romeo says and then barks orders at the others.

While the others searched the woods, he carried me back to one of the cars and takes me to an urgent care. I must have passed out on the way because when I woke up, I was laying in a hospital bed, with a hospital gown on. With monitors attached and an IV in my arm. When I tried to move, I got hit with a wave of pain from my rib cage. I looked around and Romeo was sitting in the corner. I call out to him and he jumps up when he sees that I am awake. I try to pull the leads off and get out of bed. Romeo stops me, asks me how I am feeling and pushes the button for a nurse to come in.

"Hospitals means cops, we have to get out of here." I tell him.

"Don't worry, I have a buddy that works here, he won't report it. This is a pop up clinic, meaning they don't follow all the same rules." He says quietly.

After the nurse leaves, he pulls a chair up to the side of my bed and looks at me for a moment.

"So I know you saw who Vulture was. And he shot you because of it. Either he was a bad shot or he didn't want to hurt you too badly. Who was it?" He says after a moment.

I turn my head to the side looking out the window at the rain with a tear flowing down my cheek.

"I didn't see his face. I don't know how I missed him. I must have walked right by him. I heard a twig break behind me and I turned around and he was right there. His face was in the shadows, I don't know who it was." I say looking back at him with a sigh.

"Well we have his contact, we should find out who he is pretty soon." He says disappointed.

"What about Marcus?" I ask quietly.

"He escaped, hurt one of our guys pretty bad, he's being treated in the next room. The situation is being handled." He says looking out the window.

"I'm tired, I need to get some rest." I say pulling up the blanket.

Romeo goes back to his seat and sits down. He leans forward and whispers; "You really should talk to a nurse about what happened at the party. You need to get checked out."

A few days later, Romeo and I were driving back to the apartment to pick up our stuff we had left there.

"Hey, why don't you go up and get our stuff together. I'll go fill the car up with gas and get some food. Do you want anything?" Romeo asks.

"Grab me a bag of white powdered donuts and a large milk?" I respond.

"Copy that. I'll be back and come up in about fifteen minutes." Romeo replies.

I hop out of the car and slowly climb up the stairs. David, a Raven member was standing out on the landing, smoking a cigarette. He watches me walk up the stairs and flicks the cigarette away when I reach the top, then follows me into the apartment.

"Any word on how Sage is doing?" I ask him as I walk past the kitchen.

"He's on the mend." He says after a moment.

I walk into the bedroom Romeo and I had been sharing and put an over the shoulder bag on the bed. I start to take clothes out of the closet. I figured we could separate our stuff later, I just wanted to get out of here and back home. I dropped a shirt and bend over to grab it. As I'm standing back up, in the mirror on the dresser, I can see David behind me with a large piece of wood in his hand, raised up ready to strike. I duck down as he swings and he misses. I kick him in the stomach with the bottom of my foot. He falls back and I exit the room quickly. As soon as I get through the threshold of the door, another Raven member, Liam, punches me across the jaw, knocking me to the floor. He takes the opportunity of catching me off guard and drags me to the bathroom by my hair and jacket.

"You know something about your story in the woods doesn't quite add up." Liam says as he throws me to the tiled floor.

"We are here to help you. We did our part, we got you your snitch's contact. The rest is on you." I say as I spit some blood into the toilet.

"We've been interrogating him, but so far he's been reluctant to give up any real information. So now we have some questions for you." He says as David walks in.

"I don't answer to you." I start to say, but David kicks me in the stomach.

I roll on to my side coughing and as I try to get up, I notice the tub is filled with ice water. Rolling onto my back, I kick Liam as hard as I can in the balls, he falls to his knees. I stand up and punch David, he falls back but doesn't fall. I go to leave, but he grabs my hair pulling me backwards throwing me against the sink. He goes to grab me again and I elbow him in the nose and mouth, he instantly starts to bleed. He falls backwards holding his face and I try to scramble away, but Liam catches my ankle and trips me. Jumping on top of me he manages to get my left wrist into a zip tie handcuff. He punches me in the side a few times and while I try to catch my breath he puts my other hand into the zip tie pulling it tight. He stands up and then pulls me up by my arms. David spits blood into the sink, then tears the shower curtain down, taking it into the other room. Liam takes off his shirt, tossing it into the next room on the floor, then turns around, backhand slaps me and throws me into the water. The water was freezing cold and I gasped when I hit the water, probably inhaling some water in the process. I come up for air, but only get it for a second, Liam grabs me by both sides of my shirt and pushes me down into the water for a few seconds then yanks me up. I come up coughing for air.

"Who is the snitch!" He screams at me. David walks in and closes the toilet lid then sits down on it, watching.

"I DON'T KNOW! I yell at him.

He responds to that by ramming my head into the wall and pushing me back under the water again for a few seconds then yanks me back up again. Asking the same question.

"WHO'S THE FUCKING SNITCH!" He screams.

I tell him again I don't know and he pushes me down under the water again then lets me up. I keep telling him I don't know, while wondering what's taking Romeo so long.

Liam does this routine three or four more times and I finally hear Romeo come in. I look over and he is walking into the doorway. He sees what's happening and growls out "What the fuck are you doing to her!" David goes to rush him, but only makes it to the doorway, Romeo pulls his gun and shoots David. Liam rushes forward also, lunging forward and knocks Romeo over. They both struggle and fight for the gun.

At this point, I was totally out of energy and out of breath. Sopping wet, I pull myself out of the freezing water and fall to the tile floor with a wet thud. I lay on my back and cough, as I do a little bit of water splashes out. After a moment, a gunshot went off. And a moment later Romeo comes stumbling in. He rolls me over onto my side to help with the coughing and cuts the zip ties off, then goes to get some towels. He wraps me in a large towel and carries me out to the car. He goes back up to the apartment, grabs our bag and locks the apartment door.

Once he gets back to the car, he takes off. After we get about five minutes away, he pulls out a burner phone. "I need a cleanup crew over at the apartment right now." He says into the phone. He listens to what the other person says then responds. "I don't know man. Just get a team over there and clean it up. I told you this is why you don't trust a Raven." He hangs up and throws the phone on the dash.

"How you doin' over there?" He asks me.

I just cough a couple times in response.

Chapter 39

2 weeks later

The car ride was long and quiet.

"Where are we going Kai?" He asks but I don't say anything. "You haven't said anything since you picked me up behind the grocery store in the alley." He says. I still don't say anything. We ride for a while longer, until we eventually pull over. He looks out the window and sees an event with a lot of people.

"They are having a recruiting party, with different booths for the different military branches." I start talking without looking at him.

"The military?" He asks.

"Four year deployment. Best way for you to be out of the gang's reach." I continue, but still don't look at him

"Are you serious? There has to be another option. I have a life in LA, I have a girlfriend, family, and friends." He says desperately.

"You should have thought about that before you decided to become a snitch for the Diamonds and tried to break up a marriage." I say staring through the windshield.

"Don't use that word, I'm not a snitch. Ember told me it would be easy money." He says clearly irritated.

"You're a Raven." I tell him.

"And you are a Wolf." He responds.

"You are a Raven selling out your own group to the Diamonds, a snake. Which makes you a snitch. You are not safe here anymore. Caiden, you are my brother and I love you. But if you weren't my brother, I wouldn't be protecting you and I can't in the future. So you need to get the fuck out of the car." I say finally looking at him.

"What about Vanesa? I don't see you trying to get rid of her." He says.

"No one knows about her. As far as anyone knows Vulture was alone in this. We did not get one piece of evidence on you having a female accomplice. So officially, you didn't, she doesn't exist to you anymore. She wouldn't have done any of this if it wasn't for you. She goes back to her normal life, while I keep an eye on her." I tell him.

"But I love her." He says quietly.

"She is married. What ever you two had is done. Gone. Her husband would kill you both if he found out about any of this. And probably beat the shit out of me for trying to protect the two of you. So again, get the fuck out of the car and pick a branch.

"So you think being in a war zone is safer than being around for the gang to be able to get to me." He thinks about it for a moment and continues, "Which branch?"

"Whichever calls out to you the most. It's up to you. Choose carefully, they will be deciding where you go and where you serve for the next four years. Read an entire contract before signing anything." I say seriously.

I look at him briefly and he looks like he is about to cry. Before I lose my nerve, I pull him by his neck closer to me, hug him, kiss him on the side of the head and reach across him opening his door. He gets out and walks towards the party without looking back at the car.

Chapter 40

A few days later, there was a break in rainy weather, so we had decided to have a beach day. Jay, Ty, Jade, Luca, Jessie myself and Cody, a new prospect, all met up at the beach. Walking across the hot sand, I looked out towards the water, there was a couple sail boats out in the distance. We pick a spot near one of the life guard towers. The paint on the legs of the tower slightly rusted. We put the blanket down and put four rocks down, one on each corner. It wasn't too busy, a couple groups scattered far apart across the beach. The sun was high and I could already feel the skin on my shoulders burning. Seeming to have read my mind, Jay grabs the sunscreen and motions for me to turn around as he rubs it into my skin.

The salty air hangs around us as our toes dig into the sand, the layers underneath cooler than the surface. Cody, Jade and Jessie go surfing, we watch as they catch waves while trying to teach Cody how to surf. He fails miserably but doesn't stop trying.

I look at my feet for a few moments and think to myself; *man I really need to get a pedicure.*

"Man this whole thing with the Ravens was fucked up. And to make matters worse, Romeo and Vanessa might break up over the whole Robyn thing." Ty says breaking the silence of the waves crashing and gulls screeching.

"She can't get over the fact that they used to be together and he is still around her. It also doesn't help his case that he was gone and out of reach for almost a month, Vanessa probably thinks he went to see Robyn while he was on the raid." I tell him.

That cold bitch, I think to myself, *even though she's the one who had an affair, she's blaming him. Her and I need to have a little chat.*

"I mean it's not like he can tell her all the details about the raid. That's shits top secret." Ty says.

"A lot of shit lately has been fucked up. This shits just broken, like them." I say and think to myself *broken like me*.

"I dunno, who isn't a little broken these days? Sure, maybe we are a little more fucked up than the rest, but we are all a little broken. If you look hard enough you can find beauty in the broken. Broken doesn't mean ruined, even a broken window can be fixed." Ty says.

"Broken windows are replaced, not fixed bro." Luca tells him and we all chuckle a little.

"Shit man you know what I mean." He says getting a little irritated and butt hurt that we broke up his deep thinking.

"Are you high right now bro?" Luca asks him.

"Ok, maybe a little." Ty says with a smile then continues; "Hey it's our day off, I didn't drive, Jade did." He says putting his hands up in defense.

Jay was sitting in front of me he was really quiet. Probably thinking about his brothers marriage collapsing .

But probably not, he's probably thinking about random guy stuff.

I lean forward and say in his ear, "Wanna go for a swim with me?" He smiles and gets up, offering out his hand.

"We're gonna go for a swim guys ." I tell the group and they nod.

I take off my cover up and throw it onto the blanket, leaving me in that black two piece bikini that Mira had bought me in Vegas. The guys all whistle and Jay says with a laugh, "Back off fellas, this ones taken."

We walk to the water and as we reach the waterline, the water washes over our feet. It was a little cold since we had been sitting in the sun, but it was refreshing.

"Man you are lookin sexy today." Jay says while intertwining our fingers together.
I just smile and we walk deeper into the water.

Chapter 41

A couple days later, Jessie, Ty, Taj and I were on a night delivery. Jessie and I were waiting out in his new racer hybrid car. Jessie was a street racer like me, but wasn't that great, he typically didn't win. I think he does it just for the thrill.

Ty and Taj were across the street meeting a contact exchanging a large amount of cash in two backpacks. A cop car pulls over and turns their lights off not far from where we are. I look around us and there is a rather suspicious looking black sedan sitting directly across from them.

"Shit, those must be cops in an unmarked car and they are looking right at the meeting." I say.

"Fuck, where?" Jessie asks and I point. "Shit, we have to warn them." He says.

"They don't have their phones. We can't honk that would be too obvious." I say.

As luck would have it, a familiar car I used to race is pulling up to the red light.

"Hurry, switch spots with me." I tell him.

"What? Your license is still suspended." He says.

"Do you want them to go to jail? Move over!" I tell him.

He crawls to the back seat and I move over. He climbs into the passenger seat. We both put our seat belts on.

"Please tell me you have false plates on this car." I ask as I turn the car on and pull out, then pull up next to the other car.

"Of course I do. Why?" He asks.

"You're about to find out. Put a bandana over your face." I say after putting mine on.

I start revving the engine as loud as it will go and you can feel the vibrations in your bones. I roll my window down. The other driver rolls his window down and looks at me. I pull my mask down for a split second so he recognizes me, then pull it back up. I flip him off and he smiles seeing my bandana, he knows I mean business. He puts on his own bandana and nods at me.

"Give me a cash wad out of the bag in the back." I tell Jessie.

He hands it to me and I hold it up for the other driver to see. Thousand in cash bet each. He holds up his own cash bet and I put up three fingers, which means track three so we know which direction and route to race. But also where the end spot would be; which is a local hangout for racers after we wait for three minutes in a parking garage so no cops follow us there. We nod at each other. We both roll up our windows and start revving our engines. The vibrations are so much, it rattles the windows on the buildings around us. Taj and Ty look at us for a moment then get the message. They quickly walk away from the other two guys without exchanging anything.

"Text this number and tell them to clear the runway for a finish line." I tell Jessie, handing him my phone.

I focus on the light, smoking my tires. As soon as the light turns green we peel out. We get past two lights before the cops start chasing us, their sirens wailing behind us. We drift in harmony together around the corner and then get on a straight away. We go faster and faster. He slightly pulls ahead. Just like he always did, he was going too fast for the turn and spun out. I drifted through the turn perfectly, while he tries to catch up. I blocked him from getting around me and we sped through and drifted through a few more turns and intersections. We pull into the parking garage and each set a timer for three minutes, showing them to each other through the glass. We hear the cops race right by and when the timers go off we peel out racing to the finish. As we come up on the driveway, I hit the brakes and slide into the parking lot. I beat him by a good length as we pull into the parking lot. Everyone starts cheering and whistling at us when we pull up. We park and get out of the car, you can tell Cane is pissed. But as he walks up he smiles, "I should have known better. You always beat me." He says as he hugs me.

"You still have all those bad habits, Cane." I say with a laugh.

He hands over the thousand in cash and kisses me on the cheek, then walks away. I put the cash in Jessie's glove box and walk over to some old friends. They all scream when they see me and all hug me.

1 hour later.

We were all hanging out, sitting in the back of a friend's truck bed and Nick shows up. I hop off the tailgate and stand up straight.

"Ok, now I really think you are stalking me." I tell him as he walks up

"I asked you one thing Kai. One thing. Not to screw with my business." He said. Clearly trying to stay calm.

"And I asked you to keep Marcus away from me. And you failed miserably at that." I retorted.

His prospect showed up behind him. He wouldn't make eye contact.

"What do you mean by that?" He asks.

"Why don't you ask your prospect?" I say.

"What does he have to do with this?" He says looking at him then back towards me, "Marcus said he left the party after I stopped him from following you. He got jumped on his way home and was stabbed by some tweaker in his ribs."

"Of course that's what he told you, instead of the truth." I say with a laugh.

"Then tell me." He says.

"Why don't you ask him? He was the one who watched the door." I say pointing to the prospect.

"What the fuck happened prospect?" He asks, stepping into the prospects face.

The prospect tries to step away but Nick grabs him by the front of his shirt "TELL ME NOW PROSPECT!" He screams at him.

"Marcus assaulted her." He says quietly.

Nick stumbles backwards and shakes his head trying to make sense of everything. He goes into one of the stores. He comes back a minute later dragging Marcus by the hair.

As soon as I saw him my heart beat quickened, I could feel my anger start to build up in my chest and the back of my neck went hot as my hands balled into fists. I crossed my arms across my chest, I needed to keep my composure, there was too many witnesses around.

"You tell me right now what happened the night of the party." Nick yells.

"I told you man, some tweaker jumped me trying to get my wallet." He says with a nervous look.

"The prospect already told me what really happened. TELL ME THE TRUTH NOW!" Nick screams and punches Marcus in the face. Marcus falls back against one of the cars and wipes blood off his face. Standing up, he walks towards us with a defeated laugh.

"Look man, she's just some whore who disrespected you and disrespected our club. She needed to be taught a lesson." Marcus says.

"So you did it, you raped her." Nick asks.

"Call it what you want, but I defended your honor. I did what you couldn't do because you're such a pussy!" Marcus yelled out the last part.

Without saying another word, Nick reaches into his waistband and pulls out his gun. Shooting Marcus twice in the chest and once in the neck. Blood splatters everywhere, all over everyone and everything within a ten foot radius. As it hits my cheek, it feels hot against my skin. I wipe my hand over the side of my face, looking at the blood smeared on my hand. Looking up, my ears were still ringing, everything was quiet for a moment. He falls back hitting the ground with a thud. It seemed like he fell in slow motion. Blood starts to spill out around him. Then all of a sudden my hearing came back and everyone around us is screaming while scattering everywhere.

"You idiot, there's cameras everywhere!" Another dagger member said.

I walked towards Marcus and crouched down next to him, but far enough away to not get any blood on my shoes. Tucking my hair behind my ear on one side, I put an elbow on my knee and say to him, "I guess being an asshole was a bad decision, huh?"

He starts to cough up and choke on his own blood. A friend of mine, Regina, pulled me up and away. Sirens can be heard off in the distance getting closer and closer.

"Let's go! We have to get out of here!" She says as she pulls me towards Jessie's car. Jessie, Regina, another girl, and I all get into Jessie's car. Jessie takes off and we speed away. I look back and Nick is standing over Marcus, just staring at him, the gun still in his hand.

Chapter 42

A few days later, it was late in the day when Jessie, Ty and Jade came to pick me up. It had been one of my days off, so I was surprised to see them.

"What are you guys doing here?" I asked as I opened the door.

"We have a big surprise for you. But you can't see it till we get there." Jade says.

The guys were behind her and I could tell they were really excited. So I grab my jacket and we walk to Ty's car. Jessie and I get into the back seat, while Ty and Jade sit up front.

We had been driving for thirty five minutes and I get impatient and ask, "So does anyone wanna give me a hint as to where we are going?"

Ty looks over at Jade then back at the road. Jade turns around in her seat.

"Well I was gonna wait till we got there, but we are a few minutes out so I guess I can start now. You have been with us for the past two years. We have watched you grow and roll with the punches we have thrown at you in an amazing way. So as your next step into truly becoming part of our club, we thought it only right that it's finally time for you to get inked!" Jade says excitedly as we pull into a parking lot.

I look around and while I see a lot of food places, right in front of us is a tattoo parlor. I immediately get excited. "Are you serious? This is awesome! We should call Jay, so he can experience this with me!"

"Way ahead of ya. He's already inside waiting." Ty says as we all get out of the car.

We walk into the tattoo shop and Jay was flipping through a book of tattoos. Zach, who is a tattoo artist, was cleaning up his station. He looks up and smiles at us when we walk in. He walks over and hugs me. "Are you ready to get your very first tattoo?" Zach says, while walking over to the cash register and computer. He clicks something on the computer then walks over to the end of the counter.

"Jade already paid for everything. So we just have to go back and pick a design." He says and we walk back to his office to come up with a design. He sits down at his desk and pulls a chair out for me. I sit next to him.

"So everyone in our club tends to get one of four things as our group tats.

1. The symbol on the back of our vests, a wolf face with long fur.
2. The ladies sometimes tend to get something a little lighter style, with light lines along with flowers with the wolf.
3. The third is an all black handprint with an unshaded wolf paw print in the middle.
4. And the fourth is a howling wolf head.

Which would you like?"

I immediately knew which one. "Number three. The handprint." I tell him with a smile.

"Excellent choice. And where would you like it?" He asks, handing me the design on a piece of paper.

"How about the left side of my neck, with the thumb facing out towards my throat? So it looks like one of you placed it there with your own hand." I tell him.

"Wicked cool." He says with a smile.

He holds it up to my neck and says "I think we need to make it a little smaller than this print, so it fits your neck perfectly. He adjusts it on the computer then makes a stencil while I put my hair up in a tight bun to get my hair out of the way.

Standing up, he shaves the side of my neck and then puts a purple stencil on. He stands back and looks at it and nods at me with a smile "This is gonna look so cool on you."

We walk out and Jessie, Jade, Jay and Ty come over to look at it. They all compliment me on how amazing it's gonna look. Jade, Jessie and Ty all go to sit in the waiting room. Zach said it was fine if Jay wanted to sit in a chair next to me, as long as he stayed out of Zach's way.

Zach set out all the ink cartridges and prepared the tattoo gun. Lying down on the bench, he pulls a chair up next to me then he starts. The moments before the needle hit my neck I noticed the buzzing of the tattoo gun, the music they had playing in the background, Jay squeezing my hand encouragingly. Then it hit my skin, it stung a little but it wasn't as bad as I thought it would be. Forty five minutes in, it started to get sore but I knew it would be worth it.

Jessie had bought burritos from down the walk way and everyone was eating, but Zach and I powered through and got the tattoo done. It took a total of two hours and forty five minutes to complete. "Alright, that's it you're done. Go have a look in the mirror."

I get up and walk over to the mirror on the wall. It looked awesome, beautifully done. My skin was a little red around it but only because it was so fresh, that would calm down. Everyone came over to look at it. I was so excited and gave everyone a hug. Zack put gel and a wrap on it, then gave me a print out of care instructions.

"Let's go out and celebrate!" Jessie says.

"I have stuff to do at home. But you guys go out and have a blast." Jade says.

We walk outside and Jessie, Ty and I get into Ty's car. Jay had to go to work so he couldn't join us.

Chapter 43

Several hours later, I was at a diner with Jessie, Ty and Zach. We were having a very early breakfast. We hadn't been to bed, we had been up all night, the sun wasn't even out yet. So to say we were tanked was an understatement. We were drinking, eating and laughing. I ordered a big meal with eggs, pancakes, bacon and a coffee. I was trying to sober up a little, I had an AA meeting to attend in two hours.

We were talking and laughing. Usually the hostess would have kicked us out, but since Julie was on shift she let us hang out. She was an old friend of Jay's, she actually met Dakota through him, so she knew about the club and the guys didn't make her nervous.

Towards the end of our meal, I noticed this guy kept giving us these angry looks. I pointed it out to the guys and

Jessie turns all the way around in his chair and asks the guy "Hey ya bastard, do you got a problem?"

The guy got even more upset and said to his daughter; "You see that behavior, Isabella? If you don't clean up your act, you're gonna end up just like them."

I don't know why we thought that was so hilarious like we did, but we started busting up laughing our asses off.

She giggled and rolled her eyes at him and he swept her glass off the table. Sending it flying off the table and shattering against the floor. Her face turned bright red with embarrassment.

The guys kept laughing, but I stopped, got up and walked over, while dragging a chair over with me; letting it squeal and drag against the ground. I pulled it right up next to Isabella's chair and straddled it putting my arms on the back of the backrest.

She looked at me with wide eyes and I smiled at her. Her father started to speak "That wasn't an invitation to invade our conversation and our space. Get out of here ya tramp." He spewed out.

I took out my switchblade out of my pocket, flipped it open and jammed it into the table between the plates with a thud and the plates rattled. I let it sit there and I stared at him for a moment challenging him to say another word. Wisely, he didn't. I turned my attention back to his daughter.

"Hi Isabella, is that what you like to go by?" I ask her.

"Bella is fine." She says with a gulp.

"How old are you Bella?" I ask.

"Sixteen." She responds.

"Well Bella, how bout we play a little game, called 'like me'." I ask, she nods. "So, I'm gonna ask you a series of questions. And you answer if you've done it or not."

"Sounds easy." she says quietly.

"Let's start with an easy one. Have you ever been married like me?"

"No."

"Have you ever drank alcohol like me?"

"Yes."

"Have you ever been arrested like me?"

"No."

"Have you ever snuck out like me?"

"Yes."

"Have you ever raced cars like me?"

"No." She says with a giggle.

"Have you ever held a gun before like me?"

"Yes"

"Have you ever shot someone like me?"

"No."

"Have you ever been shot like me?"

"No."

"Have you ever been in a motorcycle gang like me?"

"No."

"Do you think you are like me Bella? I'm a fucking hurricane darlin'."

"No"

"One more, has he ever hit you?" I ask her.

"No, just thrown things." She says shyly after a moment.

I take out a piece of paper and write my number down on it, then fold it in half and hand it to her. "This is my number, if you ever need help, call me. If he takes this from you, come to this diner, tell the hostess over there you want to talk to Kai. Tell her it's Bella and she will call me." She takes it, looks at for a moment, then folds it again and sticks it in her bra. Without looking at her father, I stand up, pull my knife out of the table, fold it up, put it away and walk off dragging my chair back to my table.

"Well if you'll excuse me boys, I have an AA meeting to get to."

"Well shit bitch, if you're not gonna finish your bacon, I will." Jessie says grabbing my plate.

I walk up to the front and hand Julie a fifty dollar bill. "For my meal, Bella's meal and the damage to the table." She nods and squeezes my shoulder, then walks off. I walk out of the diner and call a rideshare.

Two Hours later.

I was running late to the monthly AA meeting my probation officer required. I hopped out of the car and pushed through the revolving doors. Walking through the empty lobby, I walk down the hall and into the reception area where the meeting was being held. It was a smaller group, eight including the leader of the group all sitting in a circle, a coffee in the hands of most. I hung by the door not wanting to interrupt the person who was talking. The room was large and bright, a wall of windows on one side letting in the yellow morning light. Sounds of chirping birds and rustling trees breeze in through the open windows.

"Ah looks like we have a late comer, come join us". The group leader says when he sees me.

As I walk towards the group, I see someone familiar, so I go sit next to him. Someone else starts talking and I scoot closer to him as I sit down, he smiles.

"Nice to see you Louie, but shouldn't you be in NA, not AA?" I whisper to him.

"You gotta start somewhere. NA, AA, they are both about reform right?" He says, looking away after a moment.

"So Kai, it's been a few months since we've seen you. Have you had any luck staying sober?" The group leader speaks up.

"These meetings are a requirement from my p.o., what do you think?" I say as I look at him with a mischievous smile.

Chapter 44

On a rainy Tuesday morning I was out with Jade, Ty and Jessie. We had just finished making a delivery. Jade and Ty were making out against his car, they pulled apart when I walked up and I laughed.

"When did this happen?" I asked them.

"It's been a few weeks, we have been keeping it under wraps until we really knew there was a connection." Jade tells me.

"Well, excuse me for a minute while I grab my wallet off the passenger seat." I tell them and they move over. I walk off and as I am about to walk in the coffee shop, I turn around and yell, "Don't get too carried away over there, lovebirds." I tease.

Ty smiles and flips me off.

A few minutes later I walk out of the coffee shop, holding a tray of four coffees. Jessie is starting to walk across the street, cat calling a group of girls.

As I walk down the three steps, gunshots start to go off. I drop the tray of coffees, they seemed to fall in slow motion while I dived behind the nearest car. As I hit the ground so do the coffees. They crash against the cement, hot coffee oozing out of the broken cups.

I take a couple of deep breaths and look over to Ty and Jade. They were both crouched down behind Ty's car with their guns drawn. I whistle to them and lightly say; "Draw their fire, I'm gonna go around and have a look."

Staying crouched down, I move around the car while Ty shoots back drawing their fire away from me. I go over by the tail lights and look out. Jessie is laying out in the street, bleeding out.

Moving back towards the front of the car, Jade looks at me and says "Move on three! 1, 2, 3 MOVE!" She yells then lays down some cover fire. I jet out diving behind Ty's car.

I crouch down next to them pulling my gun out of the back of my waistband. Ty exchanges some more rounds with the other crew, then crouches down. His front seat windows shatter covering the seats and us in glass.

"Who the fuck are they?" Jade yells.

I look in the glass of a second story window above and see them. "Ravens." I tell her.

"Shit." She replies.

"Jessie's bleedin' bad. We have to get to him." I tell them.

"We can't. There's no cover." Ty says, exchanging a few more rounds.

"I have an idea, does your back seat fold down to get to the trunk?" I ask.

"Ya it does. Why?" Ty asks, while Jade lays down some more rounds.

"We need some heavier firepower. I put that high capacity shotgun in the duffle before we left." I tell him.

"We'll keep them engaged, get that gun. I'll call for back up with the ARs." Jade tells me.

I open the back door and pull a jacket over the glass on the seat, so I don't get cut up. Laying on the floor of the car, I pull the back seat down and pull the shotgun out of the bag. Crawling back out, I close the door. I'm about to go, when Ty stops me.

"You have your vest on right?" He asks and I nod. "Good. Spray wide, go for the limbs, there are too many witnesses around. Jade is gonna stay here and lay cover fire."

We bend over as we walk and stand up straight when we clear the car. I start shooting with the shotgun as we walk forward, it's loud.

BOOM

It hits a car windshield putting a large hole in it.

BOOM

It hits the door of the car and leaves another hole. I aim higher.

BOOM

It hits the side of a brick building, sending chunks of brick flying. The chunks must have hit one of them, because I hear a loud groan.

BOOM

It hits the taillights and headlights of two cars parked close together.

We reach Jessie and Ty says "Going hands on."
Meaning he won't be able to shoot as he is dragging Jessie
to safety. Jade and I cover us, as we retreat backwards.
Laying down cover fire.

We keep going 'til we are inside of a brick building
on the other side. We see some of our guys pull up and hop
out of their trucks. They have ARs in hand and take care of
business. We attend to Jessie who is in bad shape. He had
multiple holes in him, it didn't look good.

Jessie kept coughing up blood and we couldn't
determine exactly where to put pressure. Jessie was
starting to panic. We kept having to tell him 'move your
hands'.

All the sudden, he looks at me and asks me; "Have
you ever seen snow Kai?"

"What? Ya I grew up in New York." I tell him.

"Is it beautiful? I've always wanted to see snow." He tells me.

"Hey don't do that. You're gonna be ok. I will make sure you get to see snow when you are better." I tell him and he smiles at me. That haunting smile.

A couple months later

Romeo, Jay, Jessie, Ty, Jade and I drove up to big bear. Jessie had been pretty depressed since the shooting. Not wanting to get out of bed or leave his house. I get it, I mean doctors told him he would never be able to walk again. But I promised him he would see snow. We unloaded his wheelchair out of the car, then Romeo lifted him out of the car and into his wheelchair. He wheeled through the parking lot and up to the edge of a snow covered field. He stared at it for a while then looked back at us.

"Will you help me stand?" He says as he looks back at us.

"Of course bud." Romeo says.

They get him stood up and he asks, "Will you take a photo Kai?"

Made in the USA
Columbia, SC
18 September 2020

21035734R00200